Acclaim for Philip Roth

"In *Indignation* [Roth's] pow... minished. . . . Of all Roth's recent novels, ... farthest into the unknowable. In his unshowy way, with all his quotidian specificity and merciless skepticism, Roth is attempting to storm heaven—an endeavor all the more desperately daring because he seems dead certain it's not there."   —David Gates,
The New York Times Book Review

"A triumph."   —*USA Today*

"It is Roth's virtuoso skill to couple Marcus's companionable pleasure in part-time butchering with his nightmare that the knives he wields so dexterously will be used on himself."   —*The Boston Globe*

"As always, the prose is well built—sinewy and graceful—and, as always, the wit is as sharp as a German knife. There are simply no novels by Roth in which you cannot detect the hand of a master."
—*O, The Oprah Magazine*

"Terrific. . . . There's a lovely perplexedness to the writing here."   —*GQ*

"He is a master. And the short form serves the story: The shocking rush from this book comes from watching Roth expertly and quickly build up to a half-dozen final pages that absolutely deliver the kill."
—*Entertainment Weekly*

"The interplay between a life just begun and ended, impulse and reflection, college high jinks and eternity is what makes it resonate." —*People* (four stars)

"Of how many writers can it be said that they're still producing some of their best work well into their 70s? With [*Indignation*], his twenty-fourth novel, Philip Roth proves beyond any dispute that he deserves to be counted in that select group." —*BookPage*

"Mr. Roth is a master magician who can make the same old rabbits do new tricks." —*The New York Sun*

"A magnificent display of writerly talent: a lean, powerful novel with bold characters who command attention, scenes of impressive dramatic interest and comic vitality, language that blasts the reader's cozy complacency . . . and a theme that swells imperceptibly from a murmur to a satisfying roar. . . . Read *Indignation*—read it with an ear for the naked power of Philip Roth at full tilt." —*The New York Observer*

"Copies of *Indignation*, Philip Roth's ferocious little tale, ought to be handed out on college campuses along with condoms and tetanus shots. . . . Here's a novel to be witnessed as an explosion from an author still angry enough to burn with adolescent rage and wise enough to understand how self-destructive that rage can be." —*The Washington Post Book World*

"Does anybody else writing prose today sustain a conversation with the reader as beautifully as Roth, with his whirlwind of shouts, whispers, riffs and exposition? . . . Roth returns with *Indignation* and Virtuosity."

—Oscar Villalon, *Books We Like*, NPR

"*Indignation* is a glorious act of chutzpah on the part of arguably the most fearless American novelist working today." —*Fort Worth Star-Telegram*

"It's that final twist of the knife that makes the book so powerful, and leaves you feeling unstrung when you put it down." —Bloomberg News

"Roth balances the darkness with sharp, comic irony. . . . In *Indignation*, Roth has reached back to Newark to breathe new life into all the old obsessions."

—Associated Press

"Written in elegant, economical prose. . . . Intensely psychological. . . . Utterly engrossing."

—*The Times Literary Supplement* (London)

"A late masterpiece. . . . *Indignation* is Philip Roth's best novel since *The Counterlife*. . . . Intricately wrought, passionate and fascinating."

—*Financial Times*

Philip Roth

Indignation

In 1997 Philip Roth won the Pulitzer Prize for *American Pastoral*. In 1998 he received the National Medal of Arts at the White House and in 2002 the highest award of the American Academy of Arts and Letters, the Gold Medal in Fiction. He has twice won the National Book Award and the National Book Critics Circle Award. He has won the PEN/Faulkner Award three times. In 2005 *The Plot Against America* received the Society of American Historians' prize for "the outstanding historical novel on an American theme for 2003–2004." Recently Roth received PEN's two most prestigious prizes: in 2006 the PEN/Nabokov Award and in 2007 the PEN/Saul Bellow Award for achievement in American fiction. Roth is the only living American writer to have his work published in a comprehensive, definitive edition by the Library of America.

INTERNATIONAL

Indignation

Indignation

Philip Roth

Vintage International

VINTAGE BOOKS

A DIVISION OF RANDOM HOUSE, INC.

NEW YORK

FIRST VINTAGE INTERNATIONAL EDITION, NOVEMBER 2009

Copyright © 2008 by Philip Roth

The Cataloging-in-Publication Data is on file at the
Library of Congress.

Vintage ISBN: 978-0-307-38891-9

www.vintagebooks.com

Printed in the United States of America
10 9

For K. W.

ACKNOWLEDGMENTS

The Chinese national anthem appears here in a World War Two translation of a song composed by Tian Han and Nieh Erh after the Japanese invasion of 1931; there are other translations of the song extant. During World War Two it was sung around the world by those allied with China in their struggle against the Empire of Japan. In 1949 it was adopted as the national anthem of the People's Republic of China.

Much of the dialogue attributed to Marcus Messner on pages 101–103 is taken almost verbatim from Bertrand Russell's lecture "Why I Am Not a Christian," delivered on March 6, 1927, at Battersea Town Hall, London, and collected by Simon and Schuster in 1957 in a volume of essays of the same name, edited by Paul Edwards and largely devoted to the subject of religion.

The quotations on pages 167–168 are taken from chapter 19 of *The Growth of the American Republic*, fifth edition, by Samuel Eliot Morison and Henry Steele Commager (Oxford University Press, 1962).

Olaf (upon what were once knees)
does almost ceaselessly repeat
"there is some shit I will not eat"

—E. E. Cummings,
   "i sing of Olaf glad and big"

CONTENTS

Indignation

Under Morphine

ABOUT TWO AND A HALF MONTHS after the well-trained divisions of North Korea, armed by the Soviets and Chinese Communists, crossed the 38th parallel into South Korea on June 25, 1950, and the agonies of the Korean War began, I entered Robert Treat, a small college in downtown Newark named for the city's seventeenth-century founder. I was the first member of our family to seek a higher education. None of my cousins had gone beyond high school, and neither my father nor his three brothers had finished elementary school. "I worked for money," my father told me, "since I was ten years old." He was a neighborhood butcher for whom I'd delivered orders on my bicycle all through high school, except during baseball season and on the afternoons when I had to attend interschool matches as a member of the debating team. Almost from the day that I left the store—where I'd been working sixty-hour weeks for him between the time of my high school graduation in January and the start of college in September—almost from the day that I began classes at Robert Treat, my father became frightened that I would die. Maybe his fear had something to do with the war, which the U.S. armed forces, under United Nations auspices, had immediately entered to bolster the efforts of the ill-trained and underequipped South Korean army; maybe it had something to do with the heavy casualties our troops were sustaining against the Communist firepower and his fear that if the conflict dragged on as long as World War Two had, I would be drafted into the army to fight and die on the Korean battlefield as my cousins Abe and Dave had died during World War Two. Or maybe the fear had to do with his financial worries: the year before, the neighborhood's first supermarket had opened only a few blocks from our family's kosher butcher shop, and sales had begun steadily falling off, in part because of the supermarket's meat and poultry section's undercutting my father's prices and in part because of a general postwar decline in the number of families bothering to maintain kosher households and to buy kosher meat and chickens from a rabbinically certified shop whose owner was a member of the Federation of Kosher Butchers of New Jersey. Or maybe his fear for me began in fear for himself, for at the age of fifty, after enjoying a lifetime of robust good health, this sturdy little man began to develop the persistent racking cough that, troubling as it was to my mother, did not stop him from keeping a lit cigarette in the corner of his mouth all day long. Whatever the cause or mix of causes fueling the abrupt change in his previously benign paternal behavior, he manifested his fear by hounding me day and night about my whereabouts. Where were you? Why weren't you home? How do I know where you are when you go out? You are a boy with a magnificent future before you—how do I know you're not going to places where you can get yourself killed?

The questions were ludicrous since, in my high school years, I had been a prudent, responsible, diligent, hardworking A student who went out with only the nicest girls, a dedicated debater, and a utility infielder for the varsity baseball team, living happily enough within the adolescent norms of our neighborhood and my school. The questions were also infuriating—it was as though the father to whom I'd been so close during all these years, practically growing up at his side in the store, had no idea any longer of who or what his son was. At the store, the customers would delight him and my mother by telling them what a pleasure it was to watch the little one to whom they used to bring cookies—back when his father used to let him play with some fat and cut it up like "a big butcher," albeit using a knife with a dull blade—to watch him mature under their eyes into a well-mannered, well-spoken youngster who put their beef through the grinder to make chopped meat and who scattered and swept up the sawdust on the floor and who dutifully yanked the remaining feathers from the necks of the dead chickens hanging from hooks on the wall when his father called over to him, "Flick two chickens, Markie, will ya, for Mrs. So-and-So?" During the seven months before college he did more than give me the meat to grind and a few chickens to flick. He taught me how to take a rack of lamb and cut lamb chops out of it, how to slice each rib, and, when I got down to the bottom, how to take the chopper and chop off the rest of it.

And he taught me always in the most easygoing way. "Don't hit your hand with the chopper and everything will be okay," he said. He taught me how to be patient with our more demanding customers, particularly those who had to see the meat from every angle before they bought it, those for whom I had to hold up the chicken so they could literally look up the asshole to be sure that it was clean. "You can't believe what some of those women will put you through before they buy their chicken," he told me. And then he would mimic them: "'Turn it over. No, *over*. Let me see the bottom.'" It was my job not just to pluck the chickens but to eviscerate them. You slit the ass open a little bit and you stick your hand up and you grab the viscera and you pull them out. I hated that part. Nauseating and disgusting, but it had to be done. That's what I learned from my father and what I loved learning from him: that you do what you have to do.

Our store fronted on Lyons Avenue in Newark, a block up the street from Beth Israel Hospital, and in the window we had a place where you could put ice, a wide shelf tilted slightly down, back to front. An ice truck would come by to sell us chopped ice, and we'd put the ice in there and then we'd put our meat in so people could see it when they walked by. During the seven months I worked in the store full time before college I would dress the window for him. "Marcus is the artist," my father said when people commented on the display. I'd put everything in. I'd put steaks in, I'd put chickens in, I'd put lamb shanks in—all the products that we had I would make patterns out of and arrange in the window "artistically." I'd take some ferns and dress things up, ferns that I got from the flower shop across from the hospital. And not only did I cut and slice and sell meat and dress the window with meat; during those seven months when I replaced my mother as his sidekick I went with my father to the wholesale market early in the morning and learned to buy it too. He'd be there once a week, five, five-thirty in the morning, because if you went to the market and picked out your own meat and drove it back to your place yourself and put it in the refrigerator yourself, you saved on the premium you had to pay to have it delivered. We'd buy a whole quarter of the beef, and we'd buy a forequarter of the lamb for lamb chops, and we'd buy a calf, and we'd buy some beef livers, and we'd buy some chickens and chicken livers, and since we had a couple of customers for them, we would buy brains. The store opened at seven in the morning and we'd work until seven, eight at night. I was seventeen, young and eager and energetic, and by five I'd be whipped. And there he was, still going strong, throwing hundred-pound forequarters on his shoulders, walking in and hanging them in the refrigerator on hooks. There he was, cutting and slicing with the knives, chopping with the cleaver, still filling out orders at seven P.M. when I was ready to collapse. But my job was to clean the butcher blocks last thing before we went home, to throw some sawdust on the blocks and then scrape them with the iron brush, and so, marshaling the energy left in me, I'd scrape out the blood to keep the place kosher.

I look back at those seven months as a wonderful time—wonderful except when it came to eviscerating chickens. And even that was wonderful in its way, because it was something you did, and did well, that you didn't care to do. So there was a lesson in doing it. And lessons I loved—bring them on! And I loved my father, and he me, more than ever before in our lives. In the store, I prepared our lunch, his and mine. Not only did we eat our lunch there but we cooked our lunch there, on a small grill in the backroom, right next to where we cut up and prepared the meat. I'd grill chicken livers for us, I'd grill little flank steaks for us, and never were we two happier together. Yet only shortly afterward the destructive struggle between us began: Where were you? Why weren't you home? How do I know where you are when you go out? You are a boy with a magnificent future before you—how do I know you're not going to places where you can get yourself killed?

During that fall I began Robert Treat as a freshman, whenever my father double-locked our front and back doors and I couldn't use my keys to open either and I had to pound on one or the other door to be let in if I came home at night twenty minutes later than he thought I ought to, I believed he had gone crazy.

And he had: crazy with worry that his cherished only child was as unprepared for the hazards of life as anyone else entering manhood, crazy with the frightening discovery that a little boy grows up, grows tall, overshadows his parents, and that you can't keep him then, that you have to relinquish him to the world.

I left Robert Treat after only one year. I left because suddenly my father had no faith even in my ability to cross the street by myself. I left because my father's surveillance had become insufferable. The prospect of my independence made this otherwise even-tempered man, who only rarely blew up at anyone, appear as if he were intent on committing violence should I dare to let him down, while I—whose skills as a cool-headed logician had made me the mainstay of the high school debating team—was reduced to howling with frustration in the face of his ignorance and irrationality. I had to get away from him before I killed him—so I wildly told my distraught mother, who now found herself as unexpectedly without influence over him as I was.

One night I got home on the bus from downtown about nine-thirty. I'd been at the main branch of the Newark Public Library, as Robert Treat had no library of its own. I had left the house at eight-thirty that morning and been away attending classes and studying, and the first thing my mother said was "Your father's out looking for you." "Why? Where is he looking?" "He went to a pool hall." "I don't even know how to shoot pool. What is he thinking about? I was studying, for God's sake. I was writing a paper. I was reading. What else does he think I do night and day?" "He was talking to Mr. Pearlgreen about Eddie, and it got him all riled up about you." Eddie Pearlgreen, whose father was our plumber, had graduated from high school with me and gone on to college at Panzer, in East Orange, to learn to become a high school phys-ed teacher. I'd played ball with him since I was a kid. "I'm not Eddie Pearlgreen," I said, "I'm me." "But do you know what he did? Without telling anybody, he drove all the way to Pennsylvania, to Scranton, in his father's car to play pool in some kind of special pool hall there." "But Eddie's a pool shark. I'm not surprised he went to Scranton. Eddie can't brush his teeth in the morning without thinking about pool. I wouldn't be surprised if he went to the moon to play pool. Eddie pretends with guys who don't know him that he's only at their level of skill, and then they play and he beats the pants off them for as much as twenty-five dollars a game." "He'll end up stealing cars, Mr. Pearlgreen said." "Oh, Mother, this is ridiculous. Whatever Eddie does has no bearing on me. Will I end up stealing cars?" "Of course not, darling." "I don't like this game Eddie likes, I don't like the atmosphere he likes. I'm not interested in the low life, Ma. I'm interested in things that matter. I wouldn't so much as stick my head in a pool hall. Oh, look, this is as far as I go explaining what I am and am not like. I will not explain myself one more time. I will not make an inventory of my attributes for people or mention my goddamn sense of duty. I will not take one more round of his ridiculous, nonsensical crap!" Whereupon, as though following a stage direction, my father entered the house through the back door, still all charged up, reeking of cigarette smoke, and angry now not because he'd found me in a pool hall but because he hadn't found me there. It wouldn't have dawned on him to go downtown and look for me at the public library—the reason being that you can't get cracked over the head with a pool cue at the library for being a pool shark or have someone pull a knife on you because you are sitting there reading a chapter assigned from Gibbon's *Decline and Fall of the Roman Empire*, as I'd been doing since six that night.

"So *there* you are," he announced. "Yeah. Strange, isn't it? At home. I sleep here. I live here. I am your son, remember?" "Are you? I've been everywhere looking for you." "Why? Why? Somebody, please, tell me why 'everywhere.'" "Because if any-thing were to happen to you—if something were ever to happen to you—" "But nothing will happen. Dad, I am not this terror of the earth who plays pool, Eddie Pearlgreen! Nothing is going to hap-pen." "I know that you're not him, for God's sake. I know better than anybody that I'm lucky with my boy." "Then what is this all about, Dad?" "It's about life, where the tiniest misstep can have tragic con-sequences." "Oh, Christ, you sound like a fortune cookie." "Do I? Do I? Not like a concerned father but like a fortune cookie? That's what I sound like when I'm talking to my son about the future he has ahead of him, which any little thing could destroy, the tiniest thing?" "Oh, the hell with it!" I cried, and ran out of the house, wondering where I could find a car to steal to go to Scranton to play pool and maybe pick up the clap on the side.

Later I learned from my mother the full circum-stances of that day, about how Mr. Pearlgreen had come to see about the toilet at the back of the store that morning and left my father brooding over their conversation from then until closing time. He must have smoked three packs of cigarettes, she told me, he was so upset. "You don't know how proud of you he is," my mother said. "Everybody who comes into the store—'My son, all A's. Never lets us down. Doesn't even have to look at his books —automatically, A's.' Darling, when you're not present you are the focus of all his praise. You must believe that. He boasts about you all the time." "And when I *am* present I'm the focus of these crazy new fears, and I'm sick and tired of it, Ma." My mother said, "But I heard him, Markie. He told Mr. Pearlgreen, 'Thank God I don't have to worry about these things with my boy.' I was there with him in the store when Mr. Pearlgreen came because of the leak. That's exactly what he said when Mr. Pearlgreen was telling him about Eddie. Those were his words: 'I don't have to worry about these things with my boy.' But what does Mr. Pearlgreen say back to him—and this is what started him off—he says, 'Listen to me, Messner. I like you, Messner, you were good to us, you took care of my wife during the war with meat, listen to somebody who knows from it happening to him. Eddie is a college boy too, but that doesn't mean he knows enough to stay away from the pool hall. How did we lose Eddie? He's not a bad boy. And what about his younger brother—what kind of example is he to his younger brother? What did we do wrong that the next thing we know he's in a pool hall in Scranton, three hours from home! With my car! Where does he get the money for the gas? From playing pool! Pool! Pool! Mark my words, Messner: the world is waiting, it's licking its chops, to take your boy away.'" "And my father believes him," I said. "My father believes not what he sees with his eyes for an entire lifetime, instead he believes what he's told by the plumber on his knees fixing the toilet in the back of the store!" I couldn't stop. He'd been driven crazy by the chance remark of a plumber! "Yeah, Ma," I finally said, storming off to my room, "the tiniest, littlest things *do* have tragic consequences. He proves it!"

I had to get away but I didn't know where to go. I didn't know one college from another. Auburn. Wake Forest. Ball State. SMU. Vanderbilt. Muhlenberg. They were nothing but the names of football teams to me. Every fall I eagerly listened to the results of the college games on Bill Stern's Saturday evening sports roundup, but I had little idea of the academic differences between the contending schools. Louisiana State 35, Rice 20; Cornell 21, Lafayette 7; Northwestern 14, Illinois 13. *That* was the difference I knew about: the point spread. A college was a college—that you attended one and eventually earned a degree was all that mattered to a family as unworldly as mine. I was going to the one downtown because it was close to home and we could afford it.

And that was fine with me. At the outset of my mature life, before everything suddenly became so difficult, I had a great talent for being satisfied. I'd had it all through childhood, and in my freshman year at Robert Treat it was in my repertoire still. I was thrilled to be there. I'd quickly come to idolize my professors and to make friends, most of them from working families like my own and with little, if any, more education than my own. Some were Jewish and from my high school, but most were not, and it at first excited me to have lunch with them *because* they were Irish or Italian and to me a new category, not only of Newarker but of human being. And I was excited to be taking college courses; though they were rudimentary, something was beginning to happen to my brain akin to what had happened when I first laid eyes on the alphabet.

And, too—after the coach had gotten me to choke up a few inches on the bat and to punch the ball over the infield and into the outfield instead of my mightily swinging as blindly as I had in high school —I had gained a first-string position on the tiny college's freshman baseball team that spring and was playing second base alongside a shortstop named Angelo Spinelli.

But primarily I was learning, discovering something new every hour of the school day, which was why I even enjoyed Robert Treat's being so small and unobtrusive, more like a neighborhood club than a college. Robert Treat was tucked away at the northern end of the city's busy downtown of office buildings, department stores, and family-owned specialty shops, squeezed between a triangular little Revolutionary War park where the bedraggled bums hung out (most of whom we knew by name) and the muddy Passaic. The college consisted of two undistinguished buildings: an old abandoned smoke-stained brick brewery down near the industrial river-front that had been converted into classrooms and science labs and where I took my biology course and, several blocks away, across from the city's major thoroughfare and facing the little park that was what we had instead of a campus—and where we sat at noontime to eat the sandwiches we'd packed at dawn while the bums down the bench passed the muscatel bottle—a small four-story neoclassical stone building with a pillared entrance that from the outside looked just like the bank it had been for much of the twentieth century. The building's interior housed the college administrative offices and the makeshift classrooms where I took history, English, and French courses taught by professors who called me "Mr. Messner" rather than "Marcus" or "Markie" and whose every written assignment I tried to anticipate and complete before it was due. I was eager to be an adult, an educated, mature, independent adult, which was just what was terrifying my father, who, even as he was locking me out of our house to punish me for beginning to sample the minutest prerogatives of young adulthood, could not have been any more proud of my devotion to my studies and my unique family status as a college student.

My freshman year was the most exhilarating and most awful of my life, and that was why I wound up the next year at Winesburg, a small liberal arts and engineering college in the farm country of north-central Ohio, eighteen miles from Lake Erie and five hundred miles from our back door's double lock. The scenic Winesburg campus, with its tall, shapely trees (I learned later from a girlfriend they were elms) and its ivy-covered brick quadrangles set picturesquely on a hill, could have been the backdrop for one of those Technicolor college movie musicals where all the students go around singing and dancing instead of studying. To pay for my going to a college away from home, my father had to let go of Isaac, the polite, quiet Orthodox young fellow in a skullcap who'd begun to apprentice as an assistant after I started my first year of school, and my mother, whose job Isaac was supposed to have absorbed in time, had to take over again as my father's full-time partner. Only in this way could he make ends meet.

I was assigned to a dormitory room in Jenkins Hall, where I discovered that the three other boys I was to live with were Jews. The arrangement struck me as odd, first because I'd been expecting to have one roommate, and second because part of the adventure of going away to college in far-off Ohio was the chance it offered to live among non-Jews and see what that was like. Both my parents thought this a strange if not dangerous aspiration, but to me, at eighteen, it made perfect sense. Spinelli, the shortstop—and a pre-law student like me—had become my closest friend at Robert Treat, and his taking me home to the city's Italian First Ward to meet his family and eat their food and sit around and listen to them talk with their accents and joke in Italian had been no less intriguing than my two-semester survey course in the history of Western civilization, where at each class the professor laid bare something more of the way the world went before I existed.

The dormitory room was long, narrow, smelly, and poorly lit, with double-decker bunk beds at either end of the worn floorboards and four clunky old wooden desks, scarred by use, pushed against the drab green walls. I took the lower bunk under an upper already claimed by a lanky, raven-haired boy in glasses named Bertram Flusser. He didn't bother to shake my hand when I tried to introduce myself but looked at me as though I were a member of a species he'd been fortunate enough never to have come upon before. The other two boys looked me over too, though not at all with disdain, so I introduced myself to them, and they to me, in a way that half convinced me that, among my roommates, Flusser was one of a kind. All three were junior English majors and members of the college drama society. None of them was in a fraternity.

There were twelve fraternities on the campus, but only two admitted Jews, one a small all-Jewish fraternity with about fifty members and the other a nonsectarian fraternity about half that size, founded locally by a group of student idealists, who took in anyone they could get their hands on. The remaining ten were reserved for white Christian males, an arrangement that no one could have imagined challenging on a campus that so prided itself on tradition. The imposing Christian fraternity houses with their fieldstone façades and castlelike doors dominated Buckeye Street, the tree-lined avenue bisected by a small green with a Civil War cannon that, according to the risqué witticism repeated to newcomers, went off whenever a virgin walked by. Buckeye Street led from the campus through the residential streets of big trees and neatly kept-up old frame houses to the one business artery in town, Main Street, which was four blocks long, stretching from the bridge over Wine Creek at one end to the railroad station at the other. Main was dominated by the New Willard House, the inn in whose taproom alumni gathered on football weekends to drunkenly relive their college days and where, through the college placement office, I got a job Friday and Saturday nights, working as a waiter for the minimum wage of seventy-five cents an hour plus tips. The social life of the college of some twelve hundred students was conducted largely behind the fraternities' massive black studded doors and out on their expansive green lawns—where, in virtually any weather, two or three boys could always be seen tossing a football around.

My roommate Flusser had contempt for everything I said and mocked me mercilessly. When I tried being agreeable with him, he called me Prince Charming. When I told him to leave me alone, he said, "Such thin skin for such a big boy." At night he insisted on playing Beethoven on his record player after I got into bed, and at a volume that didn't seem to bother my other two roommates as much as it did me. I knew nothing about classical music, didn't much like it, and besides, I needed my sleep if I was to continue to hold down a weekend job and get the kind of grades that had put me on the Robert Treat Dean's List both semesters I was there. Flusser himself never got up before noon, even if he had classes, and his bunk was always unmade, the bedding hanging carelessly down over one side, obscuring the view of the room from my bunk. Living in close quarters with him was worse even than living with my father during my freshman year—my father at least went off all day to work in the butcher shop and, albeit fanatically, cared about my well-being. All three of my roommates were going to act in the college's fall production of *Twelfth Night*, a play I'd never heard of. I had read *Julius Caesar* in high school, *Macbeth* in my English literature survey course my first year of college, and that was it. In *Twelfth Night*, Flusser was to play a character called Malvolio, and on the nights when he wasn't listening to Beethoven after hours he would lie in the bunk above me reciting his lines aloud. Sometimes he would strut about the room practicing his exit line, which was "I'll be revenged on the whole pack of you." From my bed I would plead, "Flusser, please, could you quiet it down," to which he would respond—by shouting or cackling or menacingly whispering—"I'll be revenged on the whole pack of you" once again.

Within only days of arriving on the campus, I

began to look around the dormitory for somebody with an empty bunk in his room who would agree to have me as a roommate. That took several more weeks, during which time I reached the peak of my frustration with Flusser and, about an hour after I'd gone to bed one night, rose screaming from my bunk to yank a phonograph record of his from the turntable and, in the most violent act I'd ever perpetrated, to smash it against the wall.

"You have just destroyed Quartet Number Sixteen in F Major," he said, without moving from where he was smoking in the upper bunk, fully clothed and still in his shoes.

"I don't care! I'm trying to get to sleep!"

The bare overhead lights had been flipped on by one of the other two boys. Both of them were out of their bunk beds and standing in their Jockey shorts waiting to see what would happen next.

"Such a nice polite little boy," Flusser said. "So clean-cut. So upright. A bit rash with the property of others, but otherwise so ready and willing to be a human being."

"What's wrong with being a human being!"

"Everything," Flusser replied with a smile. "Human beings stink to high heaven."

"*You* stink!" I shouted. "You do, Flusser! You don't shower, you don't change your clothes, you never make your bed—you have got no consideration for *anyone!* You're either emoting your head off at four in the morning or playing music as loud as you can!"

"Well, I am not a nice boy like you, Marcus."

Here at last one of the others spoke up. "Take it easy," he said to me. "He's just a pain in the ass. Don't take him so seriously."

"But I've got to get my sleep!" I cried. "I can't do my work without getting my sleep! I don't want to wind up getting sick, for Christ's sake!"

"Getting sick," said Flusser, adding to the smile a small derisive laugh, "would do you a world of good."

"He's crazy!" I shouted at the other two. "Everything he says is crazy!"

"You destroy Beethoven's Quartet in F Major," said Flusser, "and *I'm* the one who's crazy."

"Knock it off, Bert," said one of the other boys. "Shut up and let him go to sleep."

"After what the barbarian has done to my record?"

"Tell him you'll replace the record," the boy said to me. "Tell him you'll go downtown and buy him a new one. Go ahead, tell him, so we can all go back to bed."

"I'll buy you a new one," I said, seething at the injustice of it all.

"Thank you," Flusser said. "Thank you so much. You really are a nice boy, Marcus. Irreproachable. Marcus the well-washed, neatly dressed boy. You do the right thing in the end, just like Mama Aurelius taught you."

I replaced the record out of what I earned waiting tables in the taproom of the inn. I did not like the job. The hours were far shorter than those I put in for my father at the butcher shop and yet, because of the din and the excessive drinking and the stink of beer and cigarette smoke that pervaded the place, the work turned out to be more tiring and, in its way, as disgusting as the worst things I had to do at the butcher shop. I myself didn't drink beer or anything else alcoholic, I'd never smoked, and I'd never tried by shouting and singing at the top of my voice to make a dazzling impression on girls—as did any number of inebriates who brought their dates to the inn on Friday and Saturday nights.

There were "pinning" parties held almost weekly in the taproom to celebrate the informal engagement of a Winesburg boy to a Winesburg girl by his presenting her with his fraternity pin for her to wear to class on the front of her sweater or blouse. Pinned as a junior, engaged as a senior, and married upon graduation—those were the innocent ends pursued by most of the Winesburg virgins during my own virginal tenure there.

There was a narrow cobblestone alleyway that ran back of the inn and the neighboring shops that fronted on Main Street, and students were in and out of the inn's rear door all evening long either to vomit or to be off alone to try to feel up their girlfriends and dry-hump them in the dark. To break up the necking sessions, every half hour or so one of the town's police cars would cruise slowly along the alleyway with its brights on, sending those desperate for an outdoor ejaculation scurrying for cover inside the inn. With rare exceptions, the girls at Winesburg were either wholesome-looking or homely, and they all appeared to know how to behave properly to perfection (which is to say, they appeared not to know how to misbehave or how to do anything that was considered improper), so when they got drunk, instead of turning raucous the way the boys did, they wilted and got sick. Even the ones who dared to step through the doorway into the alley to neck with their dates came back inside looking as though they'd gone out to the alley to have their hair done. Occasionally I would see a girl who attracted me, and while running back and forth with my pitchers of beer, I would turn my head to try to get a good look at her. Almost always I discovered that her date was the evening's most aggressively obnoxious drunk. But because I was being paid the minimum wage plus tips, I arrived promptly at five every weekend to begin setting up for the night and worked till after midnight, cleaning up, and throughout tried to maintain a professional waiterly air despite people's snapping their fingers at me to get my attention or whistling at me sharply with their fingers in their mouths and treating me more like a lackey than a fellow student who needed the work. More than a few times during the first weeks, I thought I heard myself being summoned to one of the rowdier tables with the words "Hey, Jew! Over here!" But, preferring to believe the words spoken had been simply "Hey, you! Over here!" I persisted with my duties, determined to abide by the butcher-shop lesson learned from my father: slit the ass open and stick your hand up and grab the viscera and pull them out; nauseating and disgusting, but it had to be done.

Invariably, after my nights of working at the inn, there would be beer sloshing about me in all my dreams: dripping from the tap in my bathroom, filling the bowl of my toilet when I flushed it, flowing into my glass from the cartons of milk that I drank with my meals at the student cafeteria. In my dreams, nearby Lake Erie, which bordered to the north on Canada and to the south on the United States, was no longer the tenth-largest freshwater lake on earth but the largest body of beer in the world, and it was my job to empty it into pitchers to serve to fraternity boys bellowing belligerently, "Hey, Jew! Over here!"

Eventually I found an empty bunk in a room on the floor below the one where Flusser had been driving me crazy and, after filing the appropriate papers with the secretary to the dean of men, moved in with a senior in the engineering school. Elwyn Ayers Jr. was a strapping, laconic, decidedly non-Jewish boy who studied hard, took his meals at the fraternity house where he was a member, and owned a black four-door LaSalle Touring Sedan built in 1940, the last year, as he explained to me, that GM manufactured that great automobile. It had been a family car when he was a kid, and now he kept it parked out back of the fraternity house. Only seniors were allowed to have cars, and Elwyn seemed to have his largely so as to spend his weekend afternoons tinkering with its impressive engine. After we'd come back from dinner—I took my macaroni and cheese in the cheerless student cafeteria with the other "independents" while he ate roast beef, ham, steak, and lamb chops with his fraternity brothers—he and I sat at separate desks facing the same blank wall and we did not speak all evening long. When we were finished studying, we washed up at the bank of sinks in the communal bathroom down the hall, got into our pajamas, muttered to each other, and went to sleep, I in the bottom bunk and Elwyn Ayers Jr. in the top.

Living with Elwyn was much like living alone. All I ever heard him talk about with any enthusiasm was the virtues of the 1940 LaSalle, with its wheelbase lengthened over previous models and with a larger carburetor that provided edged-up horsepower. In his quiet, flat Ohio accent, he'd make a dry crack that would cut off conversation when I felt like taking a break from studying to talk for a few minutes. But, lonely as it might sometimes be as Elwyn's roommate, I had at least rid myself of the destructive nuisance who was Flusser and could get on with getting my A's; the sacrifices my family was making to send me away to college made it imperative that I continue to get only A's.

As a pre-law student majoring in political science, I was taking The Principles of American Government and American History to 1865, along with required courses in literature, philosophy, and psychology. I was also enrolled in ROTC and had every expectation that when I graduated I would be sent to serve as a lieutenant in Korea. The war was by then into a second horrible year, with three-quarters of a million Chinese Communist and North Korean troops regularly staging massive offensives and, after taking heavy casualties, the U.S.-led United Nations forces responding by staging massive counteroffensives. All the previous year, the front line had moved up and down the Korean peninsula, and Seoul, the South Korean capital, had been captured and liberated four times over. In

April 1951 President Truman had relieved General MacArthur of his command after MacArthur threatened to bomb and blockade Communist China, and by September, when I entered Winesburg, his replacement, General Ridgway, was in the difficult first stages of armistice negotiations with a Communist delegation from North Korea, and the war looked as though it could go on for years, with tens of thousands more Americans killed, wounded, and captured. American troops had never fought in any war more frightening than this one, facing as they did wave after wave of Chinese soldiers seemingly impervious to our firepower, often fighting them in the foxholes with bayonets and their bare hands. U.S. casualties already totaled more than one hundred thousand, any number of them fatalities of the frigid Korean winter as well as of the Chinese army's mastery of hand-to-hand combat and night fighting. Chinese Communist soldiers, attacking sometimes by the thousands, communicated not by radio and walkie-talkie—in many ways theirs was still a premechanized army—but by bugle call, and it was said that nothing was more terrifying than those bugles sounding in the pitch dark and swarms of the enemy, having stealthily infiltrated American lines, cascading with weapons ablaze down on our weary men, prostrate from cold and huddled for warmth in their sleeping bags.

The clash between Truman and MacArthur had resulted, the previous spring, in a Senate investigation into Truman's firing of the general that I followed in the paper along with the war news, which I read obsessively from the moment I understood what might befall me if the conflict continued seesawing back and forth with neither side able to claim victory. I hated MacArthur for his right-wing extremism, which threatened to widen the Korean conflict into an all-out war with China, and perhaps even the Soviet Union, which had recently acquired the atomic bomb. A week after being fired, Mac-Arthur addressed a joint session of Congress; he argued for bombing Chinese air bases in Manchuria and using Chiang Kai-shek's Chinese nationalist troops in Korea, before concluding the speech with his famous farewell, vowing himself to "just fade away, an old soldier who tried to do his duty as God gave him the light to see that duty." After the speech, some in the Republican Party began to promote the vainglorious general with the patrician airs, who was already by then in his seventies, as their nominee in the '52 presidential election. Predictably, Senator Joseph McCarthy announced that the Democrat Truman's firing of MacArthur was "perhaps the greatest victory the Communists have ever won."

One semester of ROTC—or "Military Science," as the program was designated in the catalogue—was a requirement for all male students. To qualify as an officer and to enter the army as a second lieutenant for a two-year stint in the Transportation Corps after graduation, a student had to take no fewer than four semesters of ROTC. If you took only the one required semester, on graduating you would be just another guy caught in the draft and, after basic training, could well wind up as a lowly infantry private with an M-1 rifle and a fixed bayonet in a freezing Korean foxhole awaiting the bugles' blare.

My Military Science class met one and a half hours a week. From an educational perspective, it seemed to me a childish waste of time. The captain who was our teacher appeared dimwitted compared with my other teachers (who were themselves slow to impress me), and the material we read was of no interest at all. "Rest the butt of your rifle on the ground with the barrel to the rear. Hold the toe of the butt against your right shoe and on line with the toe. Hold the rifle between the thumb and fingers of your right hand . . ." Nonetheless, I applied myself on tests and answered questions in class so as to be sure I would be invited to take advanced ROTC. Eight older cousins—seven on my father's side and one on my mother's—had seen combat in World War Two, two of them lowly riflemen who'd been killed less than a decade back, one at Anzio in '43 and the other in the Battle of the Bulge in '44. I thought my chances for survival would be far better if I entered the army as an officer, especially if, on the basis of my college grades and my class standing—I was determined to become valedictorian—I was able to get transferred out of transportation (where I could wind up serving in a combat zone) and into army intelligence once I was in the service.

I wanted to do everything right. If I did everything right, I could justify to my father the expense of my being at college in Ohio rather than in Newark. I could justify to my mother her having to work full time in the store again. At the heart of my ambition was the desire to be free of a strong, stolid father suddenly stricken with uncontrollable fear for a grown-up son's well-being. Though I was enrolled in a pre-law program, I did not really care about becoming a lawyer. I hardly knew what a lawyer did. I wanted to get A's, get my sleep, and not fight with the father I loved, whose wielding of the long, razor-sharp knives and the hefty meat cleaver had made him my first fascinating hero as a little boy. I envisioned my father's knives and cleavers whenever I read about the bayonet combat against the Chinese in Korea. I knew how murderously sharp sharp could be. And I knew what blood looked like, encrusted around the necks of the chickens where they had been ritually slaughtered, dripping out of the beef onto my hands when I was cutting a rib steak along the bone, seeping through the brown paper bags despite the wax paper wrappings within, settling into the grooves crosshatched into the chopping block by the force of the cleaver crashing down. My father wore an apron that tied around the neck and around the back and it was always bloody, a fresh apron always smeared with blood within an hour after the store opened. My mother too was covered in blood. One day while slicing a piece of liver—which can slide or wiggle under your hand if you don't hold it down firmly enough—she cut her palm and had to be rushed to the hospital for twelve painful stitches. And, careful and attentive as I tried to be, I had nicked myself dozens of times and had to be bandaged up, and then my father would upbraid me for letting my mind wander while I was working with the knife. I grew up with blood—with blood and grease and knife sharpeners and slicing machines and amputated fingers or missing parts of fingers on the hands of my three uncles as well as my father—and I never got used to it and I never liked it. My father's father, dead before I was born, had been a kosher butcher (he was the Marcus I was named for, and he, because of his hazardous occupation, was missing half of one thumb), as were my father's three brothers, Uncle Muzzy, Uncle Shecky, and Uncle Artie, each of whom had a shop like ours in a different part of Newark. Blood on the slotted, raised wooden flooring back of the refrigerated porcelain-and-glass showcases, on the weighing scales, on the sharpeners, fringing the edge of the roll of wax paper, on the nozzle of the hose we used to wash down the refrigerator floor—the smell of blood the first thing that would hit me whenever I visited my uncles and aunts in their stores. That smell of carcass after it's slaughtered and before it's been cooked would hit me every time. Then Abe, Muzzy's son and heir apparent, was killed at Anzio, and Dave, Shecky's son and heir apparent, was killed in the Battle of the Bulge, and the Messners who lived on were steeped in *their* blood.

All I knew about becoming a lawyer was that it was as far as you could get from spending your working life in a stinking apron covered with blood —blood, grease, bits of entrails, everything was on your apron from constantly wiping your hands on it. I had gladly accepted working for my father when it was expected of me, and I had obediently learned everything about butchering that he could teach me. But he never could teach me to like the blood or even to be indifferent to it.

One evening two members of the Jewish fraternity knocked on the door of the room while Elwyn and I were studying and asked if I could come out to have a talk with them at the Owl, the student hangout and coffee shop. I stepped into the corridor and closed the door behind me so as not to disturb Elwyn. "I don't think I'm going to join a fraternity," I told them. "Well, you don't have to," one of them replied. He was the taller of the two and stood several inches taller than me and had that smooth, confident, easygoing way about him that reminded me of all those magically agreeable, nice-looking boys who'd served as president of the Student Council back in high school and were worshiped by girlfriends who were star cheerleaders or drum majorettes. Humiliation never touched these youngsters, while for the rest of us it was always buzzing overhead like the fly or the mosquito that won't go away. What did evolution have in mind by making but one out of a million look like the boy standing before me? What was the function of such handsomeness except to draw attention to everyone else's imperfection? I hadn't been wholly disregarded by the god of appearances, yet the brutal standard set by this paragon turned one, by comparison, into a monstrosity of ordinariness. While talking to him I had deliberately to look away, his features were so perfect and his looks that humbling, that shaming—that *significant*. "Why don't you have dinner at the house some night?" he asked me. "Come tomorrow night. It's roast beef night. You'll have a good meal, and you'll meet the broth-

ers, and there's no obligation to do anything else."
"No," I said. "I don't believe in fraternities." "Believe in them? What is there to believe in or not believe in? A group of like-minded guys come together for friendship and camaraderie. We play sports together, we hold parties and dances, we take our meals together. It can be awfully lonely here otherwise. You know that out of twelve hundred students on this campus, less than a hundred are Jewish. That's a pretty small percentage. If you don't get into our fraternity, the only other house that'll have a Jew is the nonsectarian house, and they don't have much going for them in the way of facilities or a social calendar. Look, to introduce myself—my name is Sonny Cottler." A mere mortal's name, I thought. How could that be, with those flashing black eyes and that deeply cleft chin and that helmet of wavy dark hair? And so confidently fluent besides. "I'm a senior," he said. "I don't want to pressure you. But our brothers have noticed you and seen you around, and they think you'd make a great addition to the house. You know, Jewish boys have only been coming here in any numbers since just before the war, so we're a

relatively new fraternity on campus, and still we've won the Interfraternity Scholarship Cup more times than any other house at Winesburg. We have a lot of guys who study hard and go on to med school and law school. Think about it, why don't you? And give me a ring at the house if you decide you want to come over and say hello. If you want to stay for dinner, all the better."

The following night I had a visit from two members of the nonsectarian fraternity. One was a slight, blond-haired boy who I did not know was homosexual—like most heterosexuals my age, I didn't quite believe that anyone was homosexual— and the other a heavyset, friendly Negro boy, who did the talking for the pair. He was one of three Negroes in the whole student body—there were none on the faculty. The other two Negroes were girls, and they were members of a small nonsectarian sorority whose membership was drawn almost entirely from the tiny population of Jewish girls on the campus. There was no face deriving from the Orient to be seen anywhere; everyone was white and Christian, except for me and this colored kid and a few dozen more. As for the student homosexuals among us, I had no idea how many there were.

I didn't understand, even while he was sleeping directly above me, that Bert Flusser was homosexual. That realization would arrive later.

The Negro said, "I'm Bill Quinby, and this is the other Bill, Bill Arlington. We're from Xi Delta, the nonsectarian fraternity."

"Before you go any further," I said, "I'm not joining a fraternity. I'm going to be an independent."

Bill Quinby laughed. "Most of the guys in our fraternity are guys who weren't going to join a fraternity. Most of the guys in our fraternity aren't guys who think like the ordinary male student on campus. They're against discrimination and unlike the guys whose consciences can tolerate their being members of fraternities that keep people out because of their race or their religion. You seem to me to be the sort of person who thinks that way yourself. Am I wrong?"

"Fellas, I appreciate your coming around, but I'm not going to join any fraternity."

"Might I ask why?" he said.

"I'd rather be on my own and study," I said.

Again Quinby laughed. "Well, there too, most of the guys in our fraternity are guys who prefer to be on their own and study. Why not come around and pay us a visit? We're not in any way Winesburg's conventional fraternity. We're a distinctive group, if I say so myself—a bunch of outsiders who have banded together because we don't belong with the insiders or share their interests. You seem to me to be somebody who'd be at home in a house like ours."

Then the other Bill spoke up, and with words pretty much like those uttered to me the night before by Sonny Cottler. "You can get awfully lonely on this campus living entirely on your own," he said.

"I'll take my chances," I said. "I'm not afraid of being alone. I've got a job and I've got my studies, and that doesn't leave much time for loneliness."

"I like you," Quinby said, laughing good-naturedly. "I like your certainty."

"And half the guys in your fraternity," I said, "have the same kind of certainty." The three of us laughed together. I liked these two Bills. I even liked the idea of belonging to a fraternity with a Negro in it—that *would* be distinctive, especially when I brought him home to Newark for the Messner family's big Thanksgiving dinner—but nonetheless I said, "I've got to tell you, I'm not in the market for anything more than my studies. I can't afford to be. Everything rides on my studies." I was thinking, as I often thought, especially on days when the news from Korea was particularly dire, of how I would go about maneuvering from the Transportation Corps into military intelligence after graduating as valedictorian. "That's what I came for and that's what I'm going to do. Thanks anyway."

That Sunday morning, when I made my weekly collect call home to New Jersey, I was surprised to learn that my parents knew about my visit from Sonny Cottler. To prevent my father's intruding in my affairs, I told the family as little as possible when I phoned. Mostly I assured them that I was feeling well and everything was fine. This sufficed with my mother, but my father invariably would ask, "So what else is going on? What else are you doing?" "Studying. Studying and working weekends at the inn." "And what are you doing to divert yourself?" "Nothing, really. I don't need diversions. I haven't the time." "Is there a girl in the picture yet?" "Not yet," I'd say. "You be careful," he'd say. "I will be." "You know what I mean," he'd say.

"Yep." "You don't want to get in any trouble." I'd laugh and say, "I won't." "On your own like that—I don't like the sound of it," my father said. "I'm fine on my own." "And if you make a mistake," he said, "with nobody there to give you advice and see what you're up to—then what?"

That was the standard conversation, permeated throughout with his hacking cough. On this Sunday morning, however, no sooner did I call than he said, "So we understand you met the Cottler boy. You know who he is, don't you? His aunt lives here in Newark. She's married to Spector, who owns the office supply store on Market Street. His uncle is Spector. When we said where you were, she told us that her maiden name was Cottler, and her brother's family lives in Cleveland, and her nephew goes to the same college and is president of the Jewish fraternity. And president of the Interfraternity Council. A Jew and president of the Interfraternity Council. How about that? Donald. Donald Cottler. They call him Sonny, isn't that right?" "That's right," I said. "So he came around—wonderful. He's a basketball star, I understand, and a Dean's List student. So what did he tell you?" "He made a pitch for his fraternity." "And?" "I said I wasn't interested in fraternity life." "But his aunt says he's a wonderful boy. All A's, like you. And a handsome boy, I understand." "Extremely handsome," I said wearily. "A dreamboat." "What's that supposed to mean?" he replied. "Dad, stop sending people to visit me." "But you're off there all by yourself. They gave you three Jewish roommates when you arrived, and the first thing you do, you move out on them to find a Gentile and you room with him." "Elwyn is the perfect roommate. Quiet, considerate, neat, and he's studious. I couldn't ask for anyone better." "I'm sure, I'm sure, I have nothing against him. But then the Cottler boy comes around—" "Dad, I can't take any more of this." "But how do I know what's going on with you? How do I know what you're doing? You could be doing anything." "I do one thing," I said firmly. "I study and I go to class. And I make about eighteen bucks at the inn on the weekend." "And what would be wrong with having some Jewish friends in a place like that? Somebody to eat a meal with, to go to a movie with—" "Look, I know what I'm doing." "At eighteen years of age?" "Dad, I'm hanging up now. Mom?" "Yes, dear." "I'm hanging up. I'll speak to you next Sunday." "But what about the Cottler boy—" were the last of his words that I heard.

There *was* a girl, if not yet in the picture, one that I had my eye on. She was a sophomore transfer student like me, pale and slender, with dark auburn hair and with what seemed to me an aloofly intimidating, self-confident manner. She was enrolled in my American history class and sometimes sat right next to me, but because I didn't want to run the risk of her telling me to leave her alone, I hadn't worked up the courage to nod hello, let alone speak to her. One night I saw her at the library. I was sitting at a desk up in the stacks that overlooked the main reading room; she was at one of the long tables on the reading room floor, diligently taking notes out of a reference book. Two things captivated me. One was the part in her exquisite hair. Never before had I been so vulnerable to the part in someone's hair. The other was her left leg, which was crossed over her right leg and rhythmically swaying up and down. Her skirt fell midway down her calf, as was the style, but still, from where I was seated I could see beneath the table the unceasing movement of that leg. She must have remained there like that for two hours, steadily taking notes without a break, and all I did during that time was to look at the way that hair was parted in an even line and the way she never stopped moving her leg up and down. Not for the first time, I wondered what moving a leg like that felt like for a girl. She was absorbed in her homework, and I, with the mind of an eighteen-year-old boy, was absorbed in wanting to put my hand up her skirt. The strong desire to rush off to the bathroom was quelled by my fear that if I did so, I might get caught by a librarian or a teacher or even by an honorable student, be expelled from school, and wind up a rifleman in Korea.

That night, I had to sit at my desk until two A.M.—and with the gooseneck lamp twisted down to keep the glare of my light clear of Elwyn, asleep in the upper bunk—in order to finish the home-work that I'd failed to do because of my being preoccupied with the auburn-haired girl's swing-ing leg.

What happened when I took her out exceeded anything I could have imagined in the library bath-room, had I the daring to retreat to one of the stalls there to relieve myself temporarily of my desire. The rules regulating the lives of the girls at Winesburg were of the sort my father wouldn't have minded their imposing on me. All female students, including seniors, had to sign in and out of their dormitories whenever they left in the evening, even to go to the library. They couldn't stay out past nine on weekdays or past midnight on Fridays and Saturdays, nor, of course, were they ever allowed in male dormitories or in fraternity houses except at chaperoned events, nor were men allowed inside the women's dorms other than to wait on a florally upholstered chintz sofa in the small parlor to pick up a date whom the attendant downstairs would summon on the house phone; the attendant would have gotten the young man's name from his student ID card, which he was required to show her. Since students other than seniors were prohibited from having cars on campus—and in a college with a preponderantly middle-class student body, only a few seniors had families who could provide for a car or its upkeep—there was almost no place where a student couple could be alone together. Some went out to the town cemetery and conducted their sex play against the tombstones or even down on the graves themselves; others got away with what little they could at the movies; but mostly, after evening dates, girls were thrust up against the trunks of trees in the dark of the quadrangle containing the three women's dorms, and the misdeeds that the parietal regulations were intended to curb were partially perpetrated among the elms that beautified the campus. Mainly there was no more than fumbling and groping through layers of clothing, but among the male students the passion for satisfaction even that meager was boundless. Since evolution abhors unclimactic petting, the prevailing sexual code could be physically excruciating. Prolonged excitation that failed to result in orgasmic discharge could set strapping young men to hobbling about like cripples until the searing, stabbing, cramping pain of the widespread testicular torture known as blue balls would slowly diminish and pass away. On a weekend night at Winesburg, blue balls constituted the norm, striking down dozens between, say, ten and midnight, while ejaculation, that most pleasant and natural of remedies, was the ever-elusive, unprecedented event in the erotic career of a student libidinally at his lifetime's peak of performance.

My roommate, Elwyn, loaned me his black LaSalle the night I took out Olivia Hutton. It was a weeknight, when I wasn't working, and so we had to start out early to get her back to her dormitory by nine. We drove to L'Escargot, the fanciest restaurant in Sandusky County, about ten miles down Wine Creek from the college. She ordered snails, the featured dish, and I didn't, not only because I'd never had them and couldn't imagine eating them, but because I was trying to keep the cost down. I took her to L'Escargot because she seemed far too sophisticated for a first date at the Owl, where you could get a hamburger, french fries, and a Coke for under fifty cents. Besides, as out of place as I felt at L'Escargot, I felt more so at the Owl, whose patrons were usually jammed into booths together alongside members of their own fraternities or sororities and, as far as I could tell, spoke mostly about social events of the previous weekend or those of the weekend to come. I had enough of them and their socializing while waiting tables at the Willard.

She ordered the snails and I didn't. She was from wealthy suburban Cleveland and I wasn't. Her parents were divorced and mine weren't, nor could they possibly be. She'd transferred from Mount Holyoke back to Ohio for reasons having to do with her parents' divorce, or so she said. And she was even prettier than I had realized in class. I'd never before looked her in the eyes long enough to see the size of them. Nor had I noticed the transparency of her skin. Nor had I dared to look at her mouth long enough to realize how full her upper lip was and how provocatively it protruded when she spoke certain words, words beginning with "m" or "w" or "wh" or "s" or "sh," as in the commonplace affirmation "Sure," which Olivia pronounced as though it rhymed with "purr" and I as though it rhymed with "cure."

After we'd been speaking for some ten or fifteen minutes, she surprisingly reached across the table to touch the back of my hand. "You're so intense," she said. "Relax."

"I don't know how to," I said, and though I meant it as a lighthearted, self-effacing joke, it happened to be true. I was always working on myself. I was always pursuing a goal. Delivering orders and flicking chickens and cleaning butcher blocks and getting A's so as never to disappoint my parents. Shortening up on the bat to just meet the ball and get it to drop between the infielders and the out-fielders of the opposing team. Transferring from Robert Treat to get away from my father's unreasonable strictures. Not joining a fraternity in order to concentrate exclusively on my studies. Taking ROTC dead seriously in an attempt not to wind up dead in Korea. And now the goal was Olivia Hutton. I'd taken her to a restaurant whose cost came to nearly half of a weekend's earnings because I wanted her to think I was, like her, a worldly sophisticate, and simultaneously I wanted dinner to end almost before it had begun so that I could get her into the car's front seat and park somewhere and touch her. To date, the limit of my carnality was touching. I'd touched two girls in high school. Each had been a girlfriend for close to a year. Only one had been willing to touch me back. I had to touch Olivia because touching her was the only path to follow if I was to lose my virginity before I graduated from college and went into the army. There—yet another goal: despite the trammels of convention still rigidly holding sway on the campus of a middling little midwestern college in the years immediately after World War Two, I was determined to have intercourse before I died.

After dinner, I drove out beyond the campus to the edge of town to park on the road alongside the town cemetery. It was already a little after eight, and I had less than an hour to get her back to the dormitory and inside the doors before they were locked for the night. I didn't know where else to park, even though I was fearful of the police car that patrolled the alley back of the inn pulling up behind Elwyn's car with its brights on and one of the cops coming around on foot to shine a flashlight into the front seat and to ask her, "Everything all right, Miss?" That's what the cops said when they did it, and in Winesburg they did it all the time.

So I had the cops to worry about, and the late hour—8:10—when I cut off the engine of the LaSalle and turned to kiss her. Without a fuss she kissed me back. I instructed myself, "Avoid rejection—stop here!" but the advice was fatuous, and my erection concurred. I delicately slipped my hand under her coat and unbuttoned her blouse and moved my fingers onto her bra. In response to my beginning to fondle her through the cloth cup of her bra, she opened her mouth wider and continued kissing me, now with the added enticement of the stimulus of her tongue. I was alone in a car on an unlit road with my hand moving around inside someone's blouse and her tongue moving around inside my mouth, the very tongue that lived alone down in the darkness of her mouth and that now seemed the most promiscuous of organs. Till that moment I was wholly innocent of anyone's tongue in my mouth other than my own. That alone nearly made me come. That alone was surely enough. But the rapidity with which she had allowed me to pro-ceed—and that darting, swabbing, gliding, teeth-licking tongue, the tongue, which is like the body stripped of its skin—prompted me to attempt to delicately move her hand onto the crotch of my pants. And again I met with no resistance. *There was no battle.*

What happened next I had to puzzle over for weeks afterward. And even dead, as I am and have been for I don't know how long, I try to reconstruct the mores that reigned over that campus and to re-capitulate the troubled efforts to elude those mores that fostered the series of mishaps ending in my death at the age of nineteen. Even now (if "now" can be said to mean anything any longer), beyond corporeal existence, alive as I am here (if "here" or "I" means anything) as memory alone (if "memory," strictly speaking, is the all-embracing medium in which I am being sustained as "myself"), I continue to puzzle over Olivia's actions. Is that what eternity is for, to muck over a lifetime's minutiae? Who could have imagined that one would have forever to remember each moment of life down to its tiniest component? Or can it be that this is merely the afterlife that is mine, and as each life is unique, so too is each afterlife, each an imperishable fingerprint of an afterlife unlike anyone else's? I have no means of telling. As in life, I know only what is, and in death what is turns out to be what was. You are not just shackled to your life while living it, you continue to be stuck with it after you're gone. Or, again, maybe I do, I alone. Who could have told me? And would death have been any less terrifying if I'd understood that it wasn't an endless nothing but consisted instead of memory cogitating for eons on itself? Though perhaps this perpetual remembering is merely the anteroom to oblivion. As a nonbeliever, I assumed that the afterlife was without a clock, a body, a brain, a soul, a god—without anything of any shape, form, or substance, decomposition absolute. I did not know that it was not only *not* without remembering but that remembering would *be* the everything. I have no idea, either, whether my remembering has been going on for three hours or for a million years. It's not memory that's obliviated here—it's time. There is no letup—for the afterlife is without sleep as well. Unless it's all sleep, and the dream of a past forever gone is with the deceased one forever. But dream or no dream, here there is nothing to think about but the bygone life. Does that make "here" hell? Or heaven? Better than oblivion or worse? You would imagine that at least in death uncertainty would vanish. But inasmuch as I have no idea where I am, what I am, or how long I am to remain in this state, uncertainty appears to be enduring. This is surely not the spacious heaven of the religious imagination, where all of us good people are together again, happy as can be because the sword of death is no longer hanging over our heads. For the record, I have a strong suspicion that you can die here too. You can't go forward here, that's for sure. There are no doors. There are no days. The direction (for now?) is only back. And the judgment is endless, though not because some deity judges you, but because your actions are naggingly being judged for all time by yourself.

If you ask how this can be—memory upon memory, nothing but memory—of course I can't answer, and not because neither a "you" nor an "I" exists, any more than do a "here" and a "now," but because all that exists is the recollected past, not recovered, mind you, not relived in the immediacy of the realm of sensation, but merely replayed. And how much more of my past can I take? Retelling my own story to myself round the clock in a clockless world, lurking disembodied in this memory grotto, I *feel* as though I've been at it for a million years. Is this really to go on and on—my nineteen little years forever while everything else is absent, my nineteen little years inescapably here, persistently present, while everything that went into making real the nineteen years, while everything that put one squarely *in the midst of*, remains a phantasm far, far away?

I could not believe then—ridiculously enough, I cannot still—that what happened next happened because Olivia wanted it to happen. That was not the way it went between a conventionally brought-up boy and a nice well-bred girl when I was alive and it was 1951 and, for the third time in just over half a century, America was at war again. I certainly could never believe that what happened might have anything to do with her finding me attractive, let alone desirable. What girl found a boy "desirable" at Winesburg College? I for one had never heard of such feelings existing among the girls of Winesburg or Newark or anywhere else. As far as I knew, girls didn't get fired up with desire like that; they got fired up by limits, by prohibitions, by outright taboos, all of which helped to serve what was, after all, the overriding ambition of most of the coeds who were my contemporaries at Winesburg: to reestablish with a reliable young wage earner the very sort of family life from which they had temporarily been separated by attending college, and to do so as rapidly as possible.

Nor could I believe that what Olivia did she did because she enjoyed doing it. The thought was too astonishing even for an open-minded, intelligent boy like me. No, what happened could only be a consequence of something being wrong with her, though not necessarily a moral or intellectual failing—in class she struck me as mentally superior to any girl I'd ever known, and nothing at dinner had led me to believe that her character was anything but solid through and through. No, what she did would have to have been caused by an abnormality. "It's because her parents are divorced," I told myself. There was no other explanation for an enigma so profound.

When I got to the room later, Elwyn was still studying. I gave him back the keys to the LaSalle, and he accepted them while continuing to underline the text in one of his engineering books. He was wearing his pajama bottoms and a T-shirt, and four empty Coke bottles stood upright beside him on the desk. He'd go through another four at least before packing it in around midnight. I wasn't surprised by his not asking me about my date—he himself never went on dates and never attended his fraternity's social events. He had been a high school wrestler in Cincinnati but had given up sports in college to pursue his engineering degree. His father owned a tugboat company on the Ohio River, and his plan was to succeed his father someday as head of the firm. In pursuit of that goal he was even more single-minded than I was.

But how could I wash and get into my pajamas

and go to sleep and say nothing to anyone about something so extraordinary having happened to me? Yet that's what I set out to do, and almost succeeded in doing, until, after lying in my bunk for about a quarter of an hour while Elwyn remained studying at his desk, I bolted upright to announce, "She blew me."

"Uh-huh," Elwyn said without turning his head from the page he was studying.

"I got sucked off."

"Yep," said Elwyn in due time, teasing out the syllable to signal that his attention was going to remain on his work regardless of what I might take it in my head to start going on about.

"I didn't even ask for it," I said. "I wouldn't have dreamed of asking for it. I don't even know her. And she blew me. Did you ever hear of that happening?"

"Nope," replied Elwyn.

"It's because her parents are divorced."

Now he turned to look at me. He had a round face and a large head and his features were so basic that they might have been modeled on those carved by a child for a Halloween pumpkin. Altogether he was constructed on completely utilitarian lines and did not look as though he had, like me, to keep a sharp watch over his emotions—if, that is, he had any of an unruly nature that required monitoring. "She tell you that?" he asked.

"She didn't say anything. I'm only guessing. She just did it. I pulled her hand onto my pants, and on her own, without my doing anything more, she unzipped my fly and took it out and did it."

"Well, I'm very happy for you, Marcus, but if you don't mind, I've got work to do."

"I want to thank you for the car. It wouldn't have happened without the car."

"Run all right?"

"Perfect."

"Should. Just greased 'er."

"She must have done it before," I said to Elwyn. "Don't you think?"

"Could be," Elwyn replied.

"I don't know what to make of it."

"That's clear."

"I don't know if I should see her again."

"Up to you," he said with finality, and so, in silence, I lay atop my bunk bed barely able to sleep for trying to figure out on my own what to think of Olivia Hutton. How could such bliss as had befallen me also be such a burden? I who should have been the most satisfied man in all of Winesburg was instead the most bewildered.

Strange as Olivia's conduct was when I thought about it on my own, it was more impenetrable still when she and I showed up at history class and, as usual, sat beside each other and I immediately resumed remembering what she had done—and what I had done in response. In the car, I had been so taken by surprise that I had sat straight up in the seat and looked down at the back of her head moving in my lap as if I were watching someone doing it to somebody other than me. Not that I had seen such a thing done before, other than in the stray "dirty picture"—always raggedy-edged and ratty-looking from being passed back and forth between so many hundreds of horny boys' hands—that would invariably be among the prized possessions of the renegade kid at the bottom of one's high school class. I was as transfixed by Olivia's complicity as by the diligence and concentration she brought to the task. How did she know what to do or how to do it? And what would happen if I came, which seemed a strong likelihood from the very first moment? Shouldn't I warn her—if there was time enough to warn her? Shouldn't I shoot politely into my handkerchief? Or fling open the car door and spray the cemetery street instead of one or the other of us? Yes, do that, I thought, come into the street. But, of course, I couldn't. The sheer unimaginableness of coming into her mouth—of coming into anything other than the air or a tissue or a dirty sock—was an allurement too stupendous for a novice to forswear. Yet Olivia said nothing.

All I could figure was that for a daughter of divorced parents, whatever she did or whatever was done to her was okay with her. It would be some time before it would dawn on me, as it has finally (millennia later, for all I know), that whatever I did might be okay with me, too.

Days passed and I didn't ask her out again. Nor after class, when we were all drifting into the hallway, did I try to talk to her again. Then, one chilly fall morning, I ran into her at the student bookstore. I can't say that I hadn't been hoping to run into her somewhere, despite the fact that when we met in class I didn't even acknowledge her presence. Every time I turned a corner on that campus, I was hoping not only to see her but to hear myself saying to her, "We have to go on another date. I have to see you. You have to become mine and no one else's!"

She was wearing a camel's hair winter coat and high woolen socks and over her auburn hair a snug white wool hat with a fleecy, red woven ball at the top. Directly in from the out-of-doors, with red cheeks and a slightly runny nose, she looked like the last girl in the world to give anyone a blowjob.

"Hello, Marc," she said.

"Oh, yes, hi," I said.

"I did that because I liked you so much."

"Pardon?"

She pulled off her hat and shook out her hair—thick and long and not cut short with a little crimp of curls over the forehead, as was the hairdo worn by most every other coed on the campus.

"I said I did that because I liked you," she told me. "I know you can't figure it out. I know that's why I haven't heard from you and why you ignore me in class. So I'm figuring it out for you." Her lips parted in a smile, and I thought, With those lips, she, without my urging, completely voluntarily . . . And yet I was the one who felt shy! "Any other mysteries?" she asked.

"Oh, no, that's okay."

"It's *not*," she said, and now she was frowning, and every time her expression changed her beauty changed with it. She wasn't one beautiful girl, she was twenty-five different beautiful girls. "You're a hundred miles away from me. No, it's not okay with you," she said. "I liked your seriousness. I liked your maturity at dinner—or what I took to be maturity. I made a joke about it, but I liked your intensity. I've never met anyone so intense before. I liked your looks, Marcus. I still do."

"Did you ever do that with someone else?"

"I did," she said, without hesitation. "Has no one ever done it with you?"

"No one's come close."

"So you think I'm a slut," she said, frowning again.

"Absolutely not," I rushed to assure her.

"You're lying. That's why you won't speak to me. Because I'm a slut."

"I was surprised," I said, "that's all."

"Did it ever occur to you that I was surprised too?"

"But you've done it before. You just told me you did."

"This was the second time."

"Were you surprised the first time?"

"I was at Mount Holyoke. It was at a party at Amherst. I was drunk. The whole thing was awful. I didn't know anything. I was drinking all the time. That's why I transferred. They suspended me. I spent three months at a clinic drying out. I don't drink anymore. I don't drink anything alcoholic and I won't ever again. This time when I did it I wasn't drunk. I wasn't drunk and I wasn't crazy. I wanted to do it to you not because I'm a slut but because I wanted to do it to you. I wanted to give you that. Can't you understand that I wanted to give you that?"

"It seems as though I can't."

"I–wanted–to–give–you–what–you–wanted. Are those words impossible to understand? They're almost all of one syllable. God," she said crossly, "what's wrong with *you?*"

The next time we were together in history class, she chose to sit in a chair at the back of the room so I couldn't see her. Now that I knew that she had had to leave Mount Holyoke because of drinking and that she'd had then to enter a clinic for three

months to stop drinking, I had even stronger reasons to keep away from her. I didn't drink, my parents drank barely at all, and what business did I
have with somebody who, not even twenty years
old, already had a history of having been hospitalized for drinking? Yet despite my being convinced
that I must have nothing further to do with her, I
sent her a note through the campus mail:

Dear Olivia,
    You think I've spurned you because of what
happened in the car that night. I haven't. As I explained, it's because nothing approaching that
had ever happened to me before. Just as no girl
ever before has said to me anything resembling
what you said in the bookstore. I had girlfriends
whose looks I've liked and who I told how pretty
they were, but no girl till you has ever said to me
that she liked my looks or expressed admiration
for anything else about me. That isn't the way it
worked with any girl I've known before or that
I've ever heard of—which is something that I've
realized about my life only since you spoke your
mind in the bookstore. You are different from
anyone I've known, and the last thing you could
ever be called is a slut. I think you're a wonder.
You're beautiful. You're mature. You are, I ad-

mit, vastly more experienced than I am. That's what threw me. I was thrown. Forgive me. Say hello to me in class.

Marc

But she didn't say anything; she wouldn't even look my way. *She* wanted nothing further to do with *me*. I'd lost her, and not, I realized, because her parents were divorced but because mine were not.

No matter how often I told myself I was better off without her and that she drank for the same reason she'd given me the blowjob, I couldn't stop thinking about her. I was afraid of her. I was as bad as my father. I *was* my father. I hadn't left him back in New Jersey, hemmed in by his apprehension and unhinged by fearful premonitions; I had become him in Ohio.

When I phoned the dormitory, she wouldn't take my calls. When I tried to get her to talk with me after class, she walked away. I wrote again:

Dear Olivia,
Speak to me. See me. Forgive me. I'm ten years older than when we met. I'm a man.

Marc

Because of something puerile in those last three words—puerile and pleading and false—I carried the letter in my pocket for close to a week before I dropped it into the slotted box for campus mail in the dormitory basement.

I got this in return:

Dear Marcus,

I can't see you. You'll only run away from me again, this time when you see the scar across the width of my wrist. Had you seen it the night of our date I would have honestly explained it to you. I was prepared to do that. I didn't try to cover it up, but as it happened you failed to notice it. It's a scar from a razor. I tried to kill myself at Mount Holyoke. That's why I went for three months to the clinic. It was the Menninger Clinic in Topeka, Kansas. The Menninger Sanitarium and Psychopathic Hospital. There's the full name for you. My father is a doctor and he knows people there and that's where the family hospitalized me. I used the razor when I was drunk but I had been thinking about doing it for a long time, all that while I wasn't living but went from class to class acting as though I were living. Had I been sober I would have succeeded. So three cheers for ten rye and gingers—they're why I'm alive today. That, and my incapacity to carry anything out. Even suicide is beyond me. I cannot justify my existence even that way. Self-accusation is my middle name.

I don't regret doing what we did, but we mustn't do anything more. Forget about me and go on your way. There's no one around here like you, Marcus. You didn't just become a man— you've more than likely been one all your life. I can't ever imagine you as a "kid" even when you were one. And certainly never a kid like the kids around here. You are not a simple soul and have no business being here. If you survive the squareness of this hateful place, you're going to have a sterling future. Why did you come to Winesburg to begin with? I'm here *because* it's so square—that's supposed to make me a normal girl. But you? You should be studying philosophy at the Sorbonne and living in a garret in Montparnasse. We both should. Farewell, beauticious man!

Olivia

I read the letter twice over, then, for all the good it did me, shouted, "There's no one around here like you! You're no simple soul either!" I had seen her using her Parker 51 fountain pen to take notes in class—a brown-and-red tortoiseshell pen—but I had never before seen her handwriting or how she signed her name with the nib of that pen, the narrow way she formed the "O," the strange height at which she dotted the two "i"s, the long graceful upswept tail at the end of the concluding "a." I put my mouth to the page and kissed the "O." Kissed it and kissed it. Then, impulsively, with the tip of my tongue I began to lick the ink of the signature, patiently as a cat at his milk bowl I licked away until there was no longer the "O," the "l," the "i," the "v," the second "i," the "a"—licked until the upswept tail was completely gone. I had drunk her writing. I had eaten her name. I had all I could do not to eat the whole thing.

That night I couldn't concentrate on my homework but remained riveted by her letter, read it again and again, read it from top to bottom, then from bottom to top, starting with "beauticious man" and ending with "I can't see you." Finally I interrupted Elwyn at his desk and asked him if he would read it and tell me what he thought. He was my roommate, after all, in whose company I spent hours studying and sleeping. I said, "I've never gotten a letter like this." That was the bewildering refrain all through that last year of my life: never before anything like this. Giving such a letter to El-wyn—Elwyn who wanted to operate a tugboat company on the Ohio River—was, of course, a big and very stupid mistake.

"This the one that blew you?" he said when he finished.

"Well—yes."

"In the car?"

"Well, you know that—yes."

"Great," he said. "All I need is for a cunt like that to slit her wrists in my LaSalle."

I was enraged by his calling Olivia a cunt and determined then and there to find a new room and a new roommate. It took a week for me to discover a vacancy on the top floor of Neil Hall, the oldest residence on the campus, dating from the school's beginnings as a Baptist seminary, and despite its exterior fire escapes, a building commonly referred to as The Firetrap. The room I found had been vacant for years before I again filed the appropriate papers with the secretary of the dean of men and moved in. It was tiny, at the far end of a hallway with a creaky wooden floor and a high, narrow dormer window that looked as though it hadn't been washed since Neil Hall was built, the year after the Civil War.

I had wanted to pack and leave my Jenkins Hall room without having to see Elwyn and explain to him why I was going. I wanted to disappear and never endure those silences of his again. I couldn't stand his silence and I couldn't stand what little he said—and how grudgingly he said it—when he deigned to speak. I hadn't realized how much I had disliked him even before he had called Olivia a cunt. The unbroken silences would make me think that he disapproved of me for some reason—because I was a Jew, because I wasn't an engineering student, because I wasn't a fraternity boy, because I wasn't interested in tinkering with car engines or manning tugboats, because I wasn't whatever else I wasn't—or that he just didn't care if I existed. Yes, he had loaned me his treasured LaSalle when I'd asked, which did momentarily seem to suggest that there was more fellow feeling between us than he was able or willing to make visible to me, or maybe just that he was sufficiently human to sometimes do something expansive and unexpected. But then he'd called Olivia a cunt, and I despised him for it.

Olivia Hutton was a wonderful girl who'd some-how become a drunk at Mount Holyoke and had tragically tried to end her life with a razor blade. She wasn't a cunt. She was a heroine.

I was still packing my two suitcases when Elwyn unexpectedly appeared in the room in the middle of the day, walked right by me, gathered up two books from the end of his desk, and turned and started back out the door, as usual without saying anything.

"I'm moving," I told him.

"So?"

"Oh, fuck you," I said.

He set down the books and punched me in the jaw. I felt as if I were going to collapse, then as if I were going to be sick, then, holding my face where he'd struck me, to see whether I was bleeding or the bone was broken or the teeth were knocked out, I watched as he picked up the two books and made his exit.

I didn't understand Elwyn, didn't understand Flusser, didn't understand my father, didn't under-stand Olivia—I understood no one and nothing. (Another big theme of my life's last year.) Why had a girl so pretty and so intelligent and so sophisticated wanted to die at the age of nineteen? Why had she become a drunk at Mount Holyoke? Why had she wanted to blow me? To "give" me something, as she put it? No, there was more than that to what she'd done, but what that might be I couldn't grasp. Everything couldn't be accounted for by her parents' divorce. And what difference would it make if it could? The more chagrined I became thinking about her, the more I wanted her; the more my jaw hurt, the more I wanted her. Defending her honor, I had been punched in the face for the first time in my life, and she didn't know it. I was moving into Neil Hall because of her, and she didn't know that either. I was in love with her, and she didn't know that—I had only just found out myself. (Another theme: only just finding things out.) I had fallen in love with an ex–teenage drunk and inmate of a psychiatric sanitarium who'd failed at suicide with a razor blade, a daughter of divorced parents, and a Gentile to boot. I had fallen in love with—or I had fallen in love with the folly of falling in love with—the very girl my father must have been imagining me in bed with on that first night he'd locked me out of the house.

Dear Olivia,

I did see the scar at dinner. It wasn't hard to figure out how it got there. I didn't say anything, because if you didn't care to talk about it, why should I? I also surmised, when you told me that you didn't want anything to drink, that you were someone who once used to drink too much. Nothing in your letter comes as a surprise.

I would very much like it if we could at least get together to take a walk—

I was going to write "to take a walk down by Wine Creek" but didn't, for fear that she would think I was perversely suggesting that she might want to jump in. I didn't know what I was doing by lying to her about noticing the scar and then compounding the lie by saying I'd doped out her drinking all on my own. Until she'd told me of the drinking in her letter, and despite the drunkenness I witnessed each weekend while working at the Willard, I'd had no idea that anyone that young could even be an alcoholic. And as for accepting with equanimity the scar on her wrist—well, that scar, which I had not noticed the night of our date, was now all I could think about.

Was this moment to mark the beginning of a lifetime's accumulation of mistakes (had I been given a lifetime in which to make them)? I thought then that it marked, if anything, the beginning of my manhood. Then I wondered if the two had co-incided. All I knew was that the scar did it. I was transfixed. I'd never been so worked up over any-one before. The history of drinking, the scar, the sanitarium, the frailty, the fortitude—I was in bondage to it all. To the heroism of it all.

I finished the letter:

> If you'd resume sitting next to me in History it would enable me to keep my mind on the class. I keep thinking of you sitting behind my back instead of thinking about what we're study-ing. I look over at the space previously occupied by your body, and the temptation to turn is a perpetual source of distraction—because, beau-ticious Olivia, I want nothing more than to be close to you. I love your looks and am nuts about your exquisite frame.

I debated whether to write "am nuts about your exquisite frame, scar and all." Would it appear in-sensitive of me to be making light of her scar, or would it appear a sign of my maturity to be making light of the scar? To play it safe, I didn't write "scar and all" but added a cryptic P.S.—"I am moving to

Neil Hall because of a disagreement with my room-mate"—and sent the letter off through the campus mail.

She did not return to sit beside me in class but chose to remain at the back of the classroom, out of my sight. I nonetheless ran off every day at noon to my mailbox in the basement of Jenkins to see if she had answered me. Every day for a week I looked into an empty box, and when a letter finally appeared it was from the dean of men.

Dear Mr. Messner:

It has come to my attention that you have taken up residence in Neil Hall after having already briefly occupied two separate rooms in Jenkins. I am concerned about so many changes of residence on the part of a transfer student who has been at Winesburg as a sophomore for less than a semester. Will you please arrange with my secretary to come to my office sometime this week? A short meeting is in order, one that I'm sure will prove useful to both of us.

Yours sincerely,
Hawes D. Caudwell,
Dean of Men

The meeting with Dean Caudwell was scheduled for the following Wednesday, fifteen minutes after chapel ended at noon. Though Winesburg became a nonsectarian college only two decades after it was founded as a seminary, one of the last vestiges of the early days, when attending religious services was a daily practice, lay in the strict requirement that a student attend chapel, between eleven and noon on Wednesdays, forty times before he or she graduated. The religious content of the sermons had been diluted into—or camouflaged as—a talk on a high moral topic, and the speakers were not always clergymen: there were occasional religious luminaries like the president of the United Lutheran Church in America, but once or twice a month the speakers were faculty members from Winesburg or nearby colleges, or local judges, or legislators from the state assembly. More than half the time, however, chapel was presided over and the lectern occupied by Dr. Chester Donehower, the chairman of Winesburg's religion department and a Baptist minister himself, whose continuing topic was "How to Take Stock of Ourselves in the Light of Biblical Teachings." There was a robed choir of some fifty students, about two-thirds of whom were young women, and every week they sang a Christian hymn to open and close the hour; the Christmas and Easter programs featured the choir singing renditions of seasonal music and were the most popular chapels of the year. Despite the school's having by then been secularized for nearly a century, chapel was held not in any of the college's public halls but in a Methodist church, the most imposing church in town, located halfway between Main Street and the campus, and the only one large enough to accommodate the student body.

I objected strongly to everything about attending chapel, beginning with the venue. I didn't think it fair to have to sit in a Christian church and listen for forty-five or fifty minutes to Dr. Donehower or anyone else preach to me against my will in order for me to qualify for graduation from a secular institution. I objected not because I was an observant Jew but because I was an ardent atheist.

Consequently, at the end of my first month at Winesburg, after having listened to a second sermon from Dr. Donehower even more cocksure about "Christ's example" than the first, I went directly from the church back up to the campus and headed for the library's reference section to sift through the college catalogues collected there, to look for another college to transfer to, one where I could continue to be free of my father's surveillance but where I would not be forced to compromise my conscience by listening to biblical hogwash that I could not bear being subjected to. So as to be free of my father, I'd chosen a school fifteen hours by car from New Jersey, difficult to reach by bus or train, and more than fifty miles from the nearest commercial airport—but with no understanding on my part of the beliefs with which youngsters were indoctrinated as a matter of course deep in the heart of America.

To make it through Dr. Donehower's second sermon, I had found it necessary to evoke my memory of a song whose fiery beat and martial words I had learned in grade school when World War Two was raging and our weekly assembly programs, designed to foster the patriotic virtues, consisted of us children singing in unison the songs of the armed services: the navy's "Anchors Aweigh," the army's "The Caissons Go Rolling Along," the air corps' "Off We Go into the Wild Blue Yonder," the marine corps' "From the Halls of Montezuma," along with the songs of the Seabees and the WACs. We also sang what we were told was the national anthem of our Chinese allies in the war begun by the Japanese. It went as follows:

> Arise, ye who refuse to be bondslaves!
> With our very flesh and blood
> We will build a new Great Wall!
> China's masses have met the day of danger.
> Indignation fills the hearts of all of our
>   countrymen,
> Arise! Arise! Arise!
> Every heart with one mind,
> Brave the enemy's gunfire,
> March on!
> Brave the enemy's gunfire,
> March on! March on! March on!

I must have sung this verse to myself fifty times during the course of Dr. Donehower's second sermon, and then another fifty during the choir's rendering of their Christian hymns, and every time giving special emphasis to each of the four syllables that melded together form the noun "indignation."

The office of the dean of men was among a number of administrative offices lining the corridor of the first floor of Jenkins Hall. The men's dormitory, where I had slept in a bunk bed first beneath Ber-

tram Flusser and then beneath Elwyn Ayers, occupied the second and third floors. When I entered
his office from the anteroom, the dean came around
from behind his desk to shake my hand. He was
lean and broad-shouldered, with a lantern jaw,
sparkling blue eyes, and a heavy crest of silver hair,
a tall man probably in his late fifties who still
moved with the agility of the young athletic star
he'd been in three sports at Winesburg just before
World War I. There were photos of championship Winesburg athletic teams on his walls, and a
bronzed football was displayed on a stand back of
his desk. The only books in the office were the vol-
umes of the college's yearbook, the *Owl's Nest*, arranged in chronological order in a glass-enclosed
case behind him.

He motioned for me to take a seat in the chair
across from his, and while returning to his side of
the desk, he said amiably, "I wanted you to come in
so we could meet and find out if I can be of any
help to you in adjusting to Winesburg. I see by
your transcript"—he lifted from his desk a manila
folder he'd been riffling through when I entered—
"that you earned straight A's for your freshman
year. I wouldn't want anything at Winesburg to in-

terfere in the slightest with such a stellar record of academic achievement."

My undershirt was saturated with perspiration before I even sat down to stiffly speak my first few words. And, of course, I was still overwrought and agitated from just having left chapel, not only because of Dr. Donehower's sermon but because of my own savage interior vocalizations of the Chinese national anthem. "Neither do I, sir," I replied.

I had not expected to hear myself saying "sir" to the dean, though it was not that unusual for timidity—taking the form of great formality—to all but overwhelm me whenever I first had to confront a person of authority. Though my impulse wasn't exactly to grovel, I had to fight off a strong sense of intimidation, and invariably I would manage this only by speaking with somewhat more bluntness than the interview required. Repeatedly I'd leave such encounters scolding myself for the initial timidity and then for the unnecessary candor by which I overcame it and swearing in the future to answer with the utmost brevity any questions put to me and otherwise to keep myself calm by shutting my mouth.

"Do you see any potential difficulties on the horizon here?" the dean asked me.

"No, sir. I don't, sir."

"How are things going with your classwork?"

"I believe well, sir."

"You're getting all you hoped for from your courses?"

"Yes, sir."

This wasn't strictly speaking true. My professors were either too starchy or too folksy for my taste, and during these first months on campus, I hadn't as yet found any as spellbinding as those I'd had during my freshman year at Robert Treat. The teachers I'd had at Robert Treat nearly all commuted the twelve miles from New York City to Newark to teach, and they seemed to me bristling with energy and opinions—some of them decidedly and unashamedly left-wing opinions, despite prevailing political pressures—in ways these midwesterners were not. A couple of my Robert Treat teachers were Jews, excitable in a manner hardly foreign to me, but even the three who weren't Jews talked a lot faster and more combatively than the professors at Winesburg, and brought with them into the classroom from the hubbub across the Hudson an attitude that was sharper and harder and more vital all around and that didn't necessarily hide their aversions. In bed at night, with Elywn asleep in the top bunk, I thought often of those wonderful teachers I was lucky enough to have had there and whom I eagerly embraced and who first introduced me to real knowledge, and, with feelings of tenderness that were unforeseen and that nearly overwhelmed me, I thought of the friends from the freshman team, like my Italian buddy Angelo Spinelli, now all lost to me. I'd never felt at Robert Treat that there was some old way of life that everyone on the faculty was protecting, which was decidedly different from what I thought at Winesburg whenever I heard the boosters intoning the virtues of their "tradition."

"You're socializing enough?" Caudwell asked. "You're getting around and meeting the other students?"

"Yes, sir."

I waited for him to ask me to list those I had met so far, expecting he would then record their names on the legal pad in front of him—which had my name written in his script across the top—and bring them into his office to find out if I'd been telling the truth. But his response was only to pour a glass of water from a pitcher on a small table behind his desk and hand it across the desk to me.

"Thank you, sir." I sipped at the water so it wouldn't go down the wrong way and set me to coughing uncontrollably. I also flushed fiercely from realizing that just by listening to my first few answers he had been able to surmise how parched my mouth had become.

"Then the only problem is that you seem to be having some trouble settling into dormitory life," he said. "Is that so? As I said in my letter, I'm a bit concerned about your having already resided in three different dormitory rooms in just your first weeks here. Tell me in your own words, what seems to be the trouble?"

The night before I had worked out an answer, knowing as I did that my moving was to be the meeting's main subject. Only now I couldn't remember what I'd planned to say.

"Could you repeat your question, sir?"

"Calm down, son," Caudwell said. "Try a little more water."

I did as he told me. I am going to be thrown out

of school, I thought. For moving too many times I am going to be asked to leave Winesburg. That's how this is going to wind up. Thrown out, drafted, sent to Korea, and killed.

"What's the problem with your accommodations, Marcus?"

"In the room to which I was initially assigned"—yes, there they were, the words that I'd written out and memorized—"one of my three roommates was always playing his phonograph after I went to bed and I wasn't able to get my night's sleep. And I need my sleep in order to do my work. The situation was insupportable." I had decided at the last minute on "insupportable" instead of "insufferable," the adjective with which I'd rehearsed the previous night.

"But couldn't you sit down and work out a time for his playing the phonograph that was agreeable to the two of you?" Caudwell asked me. "You had to move out? There was no other choice?"

"Yes, I had to move out."

"No way of reaching a compromise."

"Not with him, sir." That's as far as I went, hoping that he might find me admirable for protecting Flusser from exposure by not mentioning his name.

"Are you often unable to reach a compromise with people whom you don't see eye to eye with?"

"I wouldn't say 'often,' sir. I wouldn't say that anything like that has happened before."

"How about your second roommate? Living with him doesn't appear to have worked out either. Am I correct?"

"Yes, sir."

"Why do you think that was so?"

"Our interests weren't compatible."

"So there was no room for compromise there either."

"No, sir."

"And now you're living alone, I see. Living by yourself under the eaves in Neil Hall."

"This far into the semester, that was the only empty room I could find, sir."

"Drink some more water, Marcus. It'll help."

But my mouth was no longer dry. I was no longer sweating either. I was angered, in fact, by his saying "It'll help," when I considered myself over the worst of my nervousness and performing as well as anybody my age could be expected to in this situation. I was angered, I was humiliated, I was resentful, and I would not even look in the direction of the glass. Why should I have to go through this interrogation simply because I'd moved from one dormitory room to another to find the peace of mind I required to do my schoolwork? What business was it of his? Had he nothing better to do than interrogate me about my dormitory accommodations? I was a straight-A student—why wasn't that enough for *all* my unsatisfiable elders (by whom I meant two, the dean and my father)?

"What about the fraternity you're pledging? You're eating your meals there, I take it."

"I'm not pledging a fraternity, sir. I'm not interested in fraternity life."

"What would you say your interests are, then?"

"My studies, sir. Learning."

"That's admirable, to be sure. But nothing more? Have you socialized with anyone at all since you've come to Winesburg?"

"I work on weekends, sir. I work at the inn as a waiter in the taproom. It's necessary for me to work to assist my father in meeting my expenses, sir."

"You don't have to do that, Marcus—you can stop calling me sir. Call me Dean Caudwell, or call me Dean, if you like. Winesburg isn't a military academy, and it's not the turn of the century either. It's 1951."

"I don't mind calling you sir, Dean." I did, though. I hated it. That's why I was doing it! I wanted to take the word "sir" and stick it up his ass for singling me out to come to his office to be grilled like this. I was a straight-A student. Why wasn't that good enough for everybody? I worked on weekends. Why wasn't that good enough for everybody? I couldn't even get my first blowjob without wondering while I was getting it what had gone wrong to allow me to get it. Why wasn't *that* good enough for everybody? What more was I supposed to do to prove my worth to people?

Promptly the dean mentioned my father. "It says here your father is a kosher butcher."

"I don't believe so, sir. I remember writing down just 'butcher.' That's what I'd write on any form, I'm sure."

"Well, that's what you did write. I'm merely assuming that he's a kosher butcher."

"He is. But that's not what I wrote down."

"I acknowledged that. But it's not inaccurate, is it, to identify him more precisely as a kosher butcher?"

"But neither is what I wrote down inaccurate."

"I'd be curious to know why you didn't write down 'kosher,' Marcus."

"I didn't think that was relevant. If some entering student's father was a dermatologist or an orthopedist or an obstetrician, wouldn't he just write down 'physician'? Or 'doctor'? That's my guess, anyway."

"But kosher isn't in quite the same category."

"If you're asking me, sir, if I was trying to hide the religion into which I was born, the answer is no."

"Well, I certainly hope that's so. I'm glad to hear that. Everyone has a right to openly practice his own faith, and that holds true at Winesburg as it does everywhere else in this country. On the other hand, under 'religious preference' you didn't write 'Jewish,' I notice, though you are of Jewish extraction and, in accordance with the college's attempt to assist students in residing with others of the same faith, you were originally assigned Jewish roommates."

"I didn't write *anything* under religious preference, sir."

"I can see that. I'm wondering why that is."

"Because I have none. Because I don't prefer to practice one religion over another."

"What then provides you with spiritual sustenance? To whom do you pray when you need solace?"

"I don't need solace. I don't believe in God and I don't believe in prayer." As a high school debater I was known for hammering home my point—and that I did. "I am sustained by what is real and not by what is imaginary. Praying, to me, is preposterous."

"Is it now?" he replied with a smile. "And yet so many millions do it."

"Millions once thought the earth was flat, sir."

"Yes, that's true. But may I ask, Marcus, merely out of curiosity, how you manage to get by in life—filled as our lives inevitably are with trial and tribulation—lacking religious or spiritual guidance?"

"I get straight A's, sir."

That prompted a second smile, a smile of condescension that I liked even less than the first. I was prepared now to despise Dean Caudwell with all my being for putting me through *this* tribulation.

"I didn't ask about your grades," he said. "I know your grades. You have every right to be proud of them, as I've already told you."

"If that is so, sir, then you know the answer to your question about how I get along without any religious or spiritual guidance. I get along just fine."

I had begun to rile him up, I could see, and in just the ways that could do me no good.

"Well, if I may say so," the dean said, "it doesn't look to me like you get along just fine. At least you don't appear to get along just fine with the people you room with. It seems that as soon as there's a difference of opinion between you and a roommate, you pick up and leave."

"Is there anything wrong with finding a solution in quietly leaving?" I asked, and within I heard myself beginning to sing, "Arise, ye who refuse to be bondslaves! With our very flesh and blood we will build a new Great Wall!"

"Not necessarily, no more than there is anything wrong with finding a solution in quietly working it out and staying. Look where you've wound up—in the least desirable room on this entire campus. A room where no one has chosen to live or has had to live for many years now. Frankly, I don't like the idea of you up there alone. It's the worst room at Winesburg, bar none. It's been the worst room on the worst floor of the worst dorm for a hundred years. In winter it's freezing and by early spring it's already a hotbox, full of flies. And that's where you've chosen to spend your days and nights as a sophomore student here."

"But I'm not living there, sir, because I don't have religious beliefs—if that is what you are suggesting in a roundabout way."

"Why is it, then?"

"It's as I explained it—" I said, meanwhile, in full voice, in my head, singing, "China's masses have met the day of danger"—"in my first room I couldn't get sufficient sleep because of a roommate who insisted on playing his phonograph late into the night and reciting aloud in the middle of the night, and in my second room I found myself living with someone whose conduct I considered intolerable."

"Tolerance appears to be something of a problem for you, young man."

"I never heard that said about me before, sir," said I at the very instant I inwardly sang out the most beautiful word in the English language: "In-dig-*na*-tion!" I suddenly wondered what it was in Chinese. I wanted to learn it and go around the campus shouting it at the top of my lungs.

"There appear to be several things you've never heard about yourself before," he replied. "But 'before' you were living at home, in the bosom of your childhood family. Now you're living as an adult on his own with twelve hundred others, and what there is for you to master here at Winesburg, aside from mastering your studies, is to learn how to get along with people and how to extend tolerance to people who are not carbon copies of yourself."

Stirred up now by my stealthy singing, I blurted out, "Then how about extending some tolerance to me? I'm sorry, sir, I don't mean to be brash or insolent. But," and, to my own astonishment, leaning forward, I hammered the side of my fist on his desk, "exactly what is the crime I've committed? So I've moved a couple of times, I've moved from one dorm room to another—is that considered a crime at Winesburg College? That makes me into a culprit?"

Here he poured some water and himself took a long drink. Oh, if only I could have graciously poured it for him. If only I could have handed him the glass and said, "Calm down, Dean. Try this, why don't you?"

Smiling generously, he said, "Has anyone said it

is a crime, Marcus? You display a fondness for dramatic exaggeration. It doesn't serve you well and is a characteristic you might want to reflect upon. Now tell me, how do you get along with your family? Is everything all right at home between your mother and your father and you? I see from the form here, where you say you have no religious preference, that you also say you have no siblings. There's the three of you at home, if I'm to take what you've written here to be accurate."

"Why wouldn't it be accurate, sir?" Shut up, I told myself. Shut up, and from here on out, stop marching on! Only I couldn't. I couldn't because the fondness for exaggeration wasn't mine but the dean's: this meeting was itself based on his giving a ridiculously exaggerated importance to where I chose to live. "I was accurate when I wrote that my father was a butcher," I said. "He is a butcher. It isn't I alone who would describe him as a butcher. He would describe himself as a butcher. It's you who described him as a kosher butcher. Which is fine with me. But that's not grounds for intimating that I've been in any way inaccurate in filling out my application form for Winesburg. It was not inaccurate for me to leave the religious-preference slot blank—"

"If I may interrupt, Marcus. How do you three get along, from your perspective? That's the question I asked. You, your mother, and your father—how do you get along? A straight answer, please."

"My mother and I get along perfectly well. We always have. So have my father and I gotten along perfectly well for most of my life. From my last year in grade school until I started at Robert Treat, I worked part time for him at the butcher shop. We were as close as a son and father could be. Of late there's been some strain between us that's made us both unhappy."

"Strain over what, may I ask?"

"He's been unnecessarily worried about my independence."

"Unnecessarily because he has no reason to be?"

"None at all."

"Is he worried, for instance, about your inability to adjust to your roommates here at Winesburg?"

"I haven't told him about my roommates. I didn't think it was that important. Nor is 'inability to adjust' a proper way to describe the difficulty, sir. I don't want to be distracted from my studies by superfluous problems."

"I wouldn't consider your moving twice in less

than two months a superfluous problem, and neither would your father, I'm sure, if he were ap-
prised of the situation—as he has every right to be,
by the way. I don't think you would have bothered
moving to begin with if you yourself saw it merely
as a 'superfluous problem.' But be that as it may,
Marcus, have you gone on any dates since you've
been at Winesburg?"

I flushed. "Arise, ye who refuse—" "Yes," I said.
"A few? Some? Many?"
"One."
"Just one."

Before he could dare to ask me with whom, before I had to speak her name and be pressed to answer a single question about what had transpired
between the two of us, I rose from my chair. "Sir,"
I said, "I object to being interrogated like this. I
don't see the purpose of it. I don't see why I should
be expected to answer questions about my relations
with my roommates or my association with my religion or my appraisal of anyone else's religion.
Those are my own private affair, as is my social life
and how I conduct it. I am breaking no laws, my
behavior is causing no one any injury or harm, and
in nothing that I've done have I impinged on any-

one's rights. If anyone's rights are being impinged on, they are mine."

"Sit down again, please, and explain yourself."

I sat, and this time, on my own initiative, drank deeply from my glass of water. This was now beginning to be more than I could take, yet how could I capitulate when he was wrong and I was right? "I object to having to attend chapel forty times before I graduate in order to earn a degree, sir. I don't see where the college has the right to force me to listen to a clergyman of whatever faith even once, or to listen to a Christian hymn invoking the Christian deity even once, given that I am an atheist who is, to be truthful, deeply offended by the practices and beliefs of organized religion." Now I couldn't stop myself, weakened as I felt. "I do not need the sermons of professional moralists to tell me how I should act. I certainly don't need any God to tell me how. I am altogether capable of leading a moral existence without crediting beliefs that are impossible to substantiate and beyond credulity, that, to my mind, are nothing more than fairy tales for children held by adults, and with no more foundation in fact than a belief in Santa Claus. I take it you are familiar, Dean Caudwell, with the writings of Bertrand

Russell. Bertrand Russell, the distinguished British mathematician and philosopher, was last year's winner of the Nobel Prize in Literature. One of the works of literature for which he was awarded the Nobel Prize is a widely read essay first delivered as a lecture in 1927 entitled, 'Why I Am Not a Christian.' Are you familiar with that essay, sir?"

"Please sit down again," said the dean.

I did as he told me, but said, "I am asking if you are familiar with this very important essay by Bertrand Russell. I take it that the answer is no. Well, I am familiar with it because I set myself the task of memorizing large sections of it when I was captain of my high school debating team. I haven't forgotten it yet, and I have promised myself that I never will. This essay and others like it contain Russell's argument not only against the Christian conception of God but against the conceptions of God held by all the great religions of the world, every one of which Russell finds both untrue and harmful. If you were to read his essay, and in the interest of open-mindedness I would urge you to do so, you would find that Bertrand Russell, who is one of the world's foremost logicians as well as a philosopher and a mathematician, undoes with logic that is beyond dispute the first-cause argument, the natural-law argument, the argument from design, the moral arguments for a deity, and the argument for the remedying of injustice. To give you two examples. First, as to why there cannot be any validity to the first-cause argument, he says, 'If everything must have a cause, then God must have a cause. If there can be anything without a cause, it may just as well be the world as God.' Second, as to the argument from design, he says, 'Do you think that, if you were granted omnipotence and omniscience and millions of years in which to perfect your world, you could produce nothing better than the Ku Klux Klan or the Fascists?' He also discusses the defects in Christ's teaching as Christ appears in the Gospels, while noting that historically it is quite doubtful that Christ ever existed. To him the most serious defect in Christ's moral character is his belief in the existence of hell. Russell writes, 'I do not myself feel that any person who is really profoundly humane can believe in everlasting punishment,' and he accuses Christ of a vindictive fury against those people who would not listen to his preaching. He discusses with complete candor how the churches have retarded human progress and how, by their insistence on what they choose to call morality, they inflict on all sorts of people undeserved and unnecessary suffering. Religion, he declares, is based primarily and mainly on fear—fear of the mysterious, fear of defeat, and fear of death. Fear, Bertrand Russell says, is the parent of cruelty, and it is therefore no wonder that cruelty and religion have gone hand in hand throughout the centuries. Conquer the world by intelligence, Russell says, and not by being slavishly subdued by the terror that comes from living in it. The whole conception of God, he concludes, is a conception unworthy of free men. These are the thoughts of a Nobel Prize winner renowned for his contributions to philosophy and for his mastery of logic and the theory of knowledge, and I find myself in total agreement with them. Having studied them and having thought them through, I intend to live in accordance with them, as I'm sure you would have to admit, sir, I have every right to do."

"Please sit down," said the dean once more.

I did. I hadn't realized I had again gotten up. But that's what the exhortation "Arise!," stirringly repeated three successive times, can do to someone in a crisis.

"So you and Bertrand Russell don't tolerate or-ganized religion," he told me, "or the clergy or even a belief in the divinity, any more than you, Marcus Messner, tolerate your roommates—as far as I can make out, any more than you tolerate a loving, hardworking father whose concern for the well-being of his son is of the highest importance to him. His financial burden in paying to send you away from home to college is not inconsiderable, I'm sure. Isn't that so?"

"Why else would I be working at the New Wil-lard House, sir? Yes, that's so. I believe I told you that already."

"Well, tell me now, and this time leaving out Bertrand Russell—do you tolerate *anyone's* beliefs when they run counter to your own?"

"I would think, sir, that the religious views that are more than likely intolerable to ninety-nine per-cent of the students and faculty and administration of Winesburg are mine."

Here he opened my folder and began slowly turning pages, perhaps to renew his recollection of my record, perhaps (I hoped) to prevent himself from expelling me on the spot for the charge I had so forcefully brought against the entire college.

Perhaps merely to pretend that, esteemed and admired as he was at Winesburg, he was nonetheless someone who could bear to be contradicted.

"I see here," he said to me, "that you are studying to be a lawyer. On the basis of this interview, I think you are destined to be an outstanding lawyer." Unsmilingly now, he said, "I can see you one day arguing a case before the Supreme Court of the United States. And winning it, young man, winning it. I admire your directness, your diction, your sentence structure—I admire your tenacity and the confidence with which you hold to everything you say. I admire your ability to memorize and retain abstruse reading matter even if I don't necessarily admire whom and what you choose to read and the gullibility with which you take at face value rationalist blasphemies spouted by an immoralist of the ilk of Bertrand Russell, four times married, a blatant adulterer, an advocate of free love, a self-confessed socialist dismissed from his university position for his antiwar campaigning during the First War and imprisoned for that by the British authorities."

"But what about the Nobel Prize!"

"I even admire you now, Marcus, when you hammer on my desk and stand up to point at me so as to ask about the Nobel Prize. You have a fighting spirit. I admire that, or would admire it should you choose to harness it to a worthier cause than that of someone considered a criminal subversive by his own national government."

"I didn't mean to point, sir. I didn't even know I did it."

"You did, son. Not for the first time and probably not for the last. But that is the least of it. To find that Bertrand Russell is a hero of yours comes as no great surprise. There are always one or two intellectually precocious youngsters on every campus, self-appointed members of an elite intelligentsia who need to elevate themselves and feel superior to their fellow students, superior even to their professors, and so pass through the phase of finding an agitator or iconoclast to admire on the order of a Russell or a Nietzsche or a Schopenhauer. Nonetheless, these views are not what we are here to discuss, and it is certainly your prerogative to admire whomever you like, however deleterious the influence and however dangerous the consequences of such a so-called freethinker and self-styled reformer may seem to me. Marcus, what brings us together today, and what is worrying me today, is not your having memorized word for word as a high school debater the contrarianism of a Bertrand Russell that is designed to nurture malcontents and rebels. What worries me are your social skills as exhibited here at Winesburg College. What worries me is your isolation. What worries me is your outspoken rejection of long-standing Winesburg tradition, as witness your response to chapel attendance, a simple undergraduate requirement which amounts to little more than one hour of your time each week for about three semesters. About the same as the physical education requirement, and no more insidious, either, as you and I well know. In all my experience at Winesburg I have never come across a student yet who objected to either of those requirements as infringements on his rights or comparable to his being condemned to laboring in the salt mines. What worries me is how poorly you are fitting into the Winesburg community. To me it seems something to be attended to promptly and nipped in the bud."

I'm being expelled, I thought. I'm being sent back home to be drafted and killed. He didn't comprehend a single word I repeated to him from "Why

I Am Not a Christian." Or he did, and *that's* why I'm going to be drafted and killed.

"I have both a personal and a professional responsibility to the students," Caudwell said, "to their families—"

"Sir, I can't stand any more of this. I feel as though I'm going to vomit."

"Excuse me?" His patience exhausted, Caudwell's startlingly brilliant, crystal-blue eyes were staring at me now with a lethal blend of disbelief and exasperation.

"I feel sick," I said. "I feel as though I'm going to vomit. I can't bear being lectured to like this. I am not a malcontent. I am not a rebel. Neither word describes me, and I resent the use of either one of them, even if it's only by implication that they were meant to apply to me. I have done nothing to deserve this lecture except to find a room in which I can devote myself to my studies without distraction and get the sleep I need to do my work. I have committed no infraction. I have every right to socialize or not to socialize to whatever extent suits me. That is the long and the short of it. I don't care if the room is hot or cold—that's my worry. I don't care if it's full of flies or not full of flies. That isn't the point! Furthermore, I must call to your attention that your argument against Bertrand Russell was not an argument against his ideas based on reason and appealing to the intellect but an argument against his character appealing to prejudice, i.e., an *ad hominem* attack, which is logically worthless. Sir, I respectfully ask your permission to stand up and leave now because I am afraid I am going to be sick if I don't."

"Of course you may leave. That's how you cope with all your difficulties, Marcus—you leave. Has that never occurred to you before?" With another of those smiles whose insincerity was withering, he added, "I'm sorry if I wasted your time."

He got up from behind his desk and so, with his seeming consent, I got up from my chair as well, this time to go. But not without a parting shot to set the record straight. "Leaving is *not* how I cope with my difficulties. Think back only to my trying to get you to open your mind to Bertrand Russell. I strongly object to your saying that, Dean Caudwell."

"Well, at least we got over the 'sir,' finally . . . Oh, Marcus," he said as he was seeing me to the door, "what about sports? It says here you played for your freshman baseball team. So at least, I take it, you believe in baseball. What position?"

"Second base."

"And you'll be going out for our baseball team?"

"I played freshman ball at a very tiny city college back home. Virtually anybody who went out for the team made it. There were guys on that team, like our catcher and our first baseman, who didn't even play high school ball. I don't think I'd be good enough to make the team here. The pitching will be faster than I'm used to, and I don't think choking up on the bat, the way I did for the freshman team back home, is going to solve my hitting problem at this level of competition. Maybe I could hold my own in the field, but I doubt I'd be worth much at the plate."

"So what I understand you to be saying is that you're not going out for baseball because of the competition?"

"*No, sir!*" I exploded. "I'm not going out for the team because I'm realistic about my chances of *making* the team! And I don't want to waste the time trying when I have all this studying to do! Sir, I'm going to vomit. I told you I would. It's not my fault. Here it comes—sorry!"

I vomited then, though luckily not onto the dean or his desk. Head down, I robustly vomited onto the rug. Then, when I tried to avoid the rug, I vomited onto the chair in which I'd been sitting, and, when I spun away from the chair, vomited onto the glass of one of the framed photographs hanging on the dean's wall, the one of the Winesburg undefeated championship football team of 1924.

I hadn't the stomach to do battle with the dean of men any more than I had the stomach to do battle with my father or with my roommates. Yet battle I did, despite myself.

The dean had his secretary accompany me down the corridor to the door of the men's room, where, once inside and alone, I washed my face and gargled with water that I cupped into my hands from beneath the spigot. I spat the water into the sink until I couldn't taste a trace of vomit in my mouth or my throat, and then, using paper towels doused with hot water, I rubbed away as best I could at whatever had spattered onto my sweater, my trousers, and my shoes. Then I leaned on the sink and looked into the mirror at the mouth that I couldn't shut. I clamped my teeth together so tightly that my bruised jawbone began throbbing with pain. Why did I have to mention chapel? Chapel is a discipline, I informed my eyes—eyes that, to my astonishment, looked unbelievably fearful. Treat their chapel as part of the job that you have to do to get through this place as valedictorian—treat it the way you treat eviscerating the chickens. Caudwell was right, wherever you go there will always be something driving you nuts—your father, your roommates, your having to attend chapel forty times—so stop thinking about transferring to yet another school and just graduate first in your class!

But when I was ready to leave the bathroom for my American government class, I got a whiff of vomit again and, looking down, saw the minutest specks of it clinging to the edges of the soles of both my shoes. I took off the shoes and with soap and water and paper towels stood at the sink in my stocking feet, washing away the last of the vomit and the last of the smell. I even took my socks off and held them up to my nose. Two students came in to use the urinals just as I was smelling my socks. I said nothing, explained nothing, put my socks back on, pushed my feet into my shoes, tied the laces, and left. *That's how you cope with all your difficulties, Marcus—you leave. Has that never occurred to you before?*

I went outside and found myself on a beautiful midwestern college campus on a big, gorgeous, sunlit day, another grand fall day, everything around me blissfully proclaiming, "Delight yourselves in the geyser of life! You are young and exuberant and the rapture is yours!" Enviously I looked at the other students walking the brick paths that crisscrossed the green quadrangle. Why couldn't I share the pleasure they took in the splendors of a little college that answered all their needs? Why instead am I in conflict with everyone? It began at home with my father, and from there it has doggedly followed me here. First there's Flusser, then there's Elwyn, then there's Caudwell. And whose fault is it, theirs or mine? How had I gotten myself in trouble so fast, I who'd never before been in trouble in my life? And why was I looking for more trouble by writing fawning letters to a girl who only a year before had attempted suicide by slitting a wrist?

I sat on a bench and opened my three-ring binder and on a blank piece of lined paper I started in yet again. "Please answer me when I write to you. I can't bear your silence." Yet the weather was too beautiful and the campus too beautiful to find Olivia's silence unbearable. Everything was too beautiful, and I was too young, and my only job was to become valedictorian! I continued writing: "I feel on the verge of picking up and leaving here because of the chapel requirement. I would like to talk to you about this. Am I being foolish? You ask how did I get here in the first place? Why did I choose Winesburg? I'm ashamed to tell you. And now I just had a terrible interview with the dean of men, who is sticking his nose into my business in a way that I'm convinced he has no right to do. No, it was nothing about you, or us. It was about my moving into Neil Hall." Then I yanked the page out of the notebook as furiously as if I were my own father and tore it in pieces that I stuffed into my pants pocket. Us! There was no us!

I was wearing pleated gray flannel trousers and a check sport shirt and a maroon V-neck pullover and white buckskin shoes. It was the same outfit I'd seen on the boy pictured on the cover of the

Winesburg catalogue that I'd sent away for and received in the mail, along with the college application forms. In the photo, he was walking beside a
girl wearing a two-piece sweater set and a long, full
dark skirt and turned-down white cotton socks and
shiny loafers. She was smiling at him while they
walked together as though he'd said to her something amusingly clever. Why had I chosen Winesburg? Because of that picture! There were big leafy
trees on either side of the two happy students, and
they were walking down a grassy hill with ivy-clad,
brick buildings in the distance behind them, and
the girl was smiling so appreciatively at the boy, and
the boy looked so confident and carefree beside
her, that I filled out the application and sent it off
and within only weeks was accepted. Without telling anyone, I took from my savings account one
hundred of the dollars that I'd diligently squirreled
away of the wages I'd been paid as my father's em-
ployee, and after my classes one day I walked over
to Market Street and went into the city's biggest
department store and in their College Shop bought
the pants and shirt and shoes and sweater that were
worn by the boy in the photo. I had brought the
Winesburg catalogue with me to the store; a hun-

dred dollars was a small fortune, and I didn't want to make a mistake. I also bought a College Shop herringbone tweed jacket. In the end I had just enough change left to take the bus home.

I was careful to bring the boxes of clothing into the house when I knew my parents were off working at the store. I didn't want them to know about my buying the clothes. I didn't want anybody to know. These were nothing like the clothes that the guys at Robert Treat wore. We wore the same clothes we'd worn in high school. You didn't get a new outfit to go to Robert Treat. Alone in the house, I opened the boxes and laid the clothes out on the bed to see how they looked. I laid them out in place, as you would wear them—shirt, sweater, and jacket up top, trousers below, and shoes down near the foot of the bed. Then I pulled off everything I had on and dropped it at my feet like a pile of rags and put on the new clothes and went into the bathroom and stood on the lowered toilet seat lid so I was able to see more of myself in the medicine chest mirror than I would be able to see standing on the tile floor in my new white buckskin shoes with the pinkish rubber heels and soles. The jacket had two short slits, one on either side at the back. I'd never owned such a jacket before. Previously I'd owned two sport jackets, one bought for my bar mitzvah in 1945 and the other for my graduation from high school in 1950. Careful to take the tiniest steps, I rotated on the toilet seat lid to try to catch a look at my backside in that jacket with the slits. I put my hands in my pants pockets so as to look nonchalant. But there was no way of looking nonchalant standing on a toilet, so I climbed down and went into the bedroom and took off the clothes and put them back in their boxes, which I hid at the back of my bedroom closet, behind my bat, spikes, mitt, and a bruised old baseball. I had no intention of telling my parents about the new clothes, and I certainly wasn't going to wear them in front of my friends at Robert Treat. I was going to keep them a secret till I got to Winesburg. The clothes I'd bought to leave home in. The clothes I'd bought to start a new life in. The clothes I'd bought to be a new man in and to end my being the butcher's son.

Well, those were the very clothes on which I had vomited in Caudwell's office. Those were the clothes that I wore when I sat in chapel trying how not to learn to lead a good life in accordance with biblical teachings and singing to myself instead the Chinese national anthem. Those were the clothes I'd been wearing when my roommate Elwyn had thrown the punch that had nearly broken my jaw. Those were the clothes I was wearing when Olivia went down on me in Elwyn's LaSalle. Yes, *there's* the picture of the boy and girl that should adorn the cover of the Winesburg catalogue: me in those clothes being blown by Olivia and having no idea what to make of it.

You don't look yourself, Marcus. You all right? May I sit down?"

It was Sonny Cottler standing over me, wearing the same clothes that I was wearing, except that his wasn't an ordinary maroon pullover sweater but a maroon and gray Winesburg letter sweater that he'd earned playing varsity basketball. That too. The ease with which he wore his clothes seemed an extension somehow of the deep voice that was so rich with authority and confidence. A quiet kind of carefree vigor, an invulnerability that he exuded, repelled me and attracted me at once, perhaps because it struck me, unreasonably or not, as being rooted in condescension. His seemingly being deficient in nothing left me oddly with the impression of someone who was actually deficient in everything. But then these impressions could have been no more than the offshoot of a sophomore's envy and awe.

"Of course," I answered. "Sure. Sit."

"You look like you've been through the wringer," he said.

He, of course, looked like he'd just finished shooting a scene on the MGM lot opposite Ava Gardner. "The dean called me in. We had a disagreement. We had an altercation." Keep your mouth shut! I told myself. Why tell him? But I had to tell someone, didn't I? I had to talk to someone at this place, and Cottler wasn't necessarily a bad guy because my father had arranged for him to come to visit me in my room. Anyway, I felt so misunderstood all around that I might have looked up at the sky and howled like a dog if he hadn't happened by.

As calmly as I could, I told him about the dispute over chapel attendance between the dean and me.

"But," Cottler asked, "who goes to chapel? You pay somebody to go for you and you never have to go anywhere near chapel."

"Is that what *you* do?"

He laughed softly. "What else *would* I do? I went one time. I went in my freshman year. It was when they had a rabbi. They have a Catholic priest once each semester, and they have a rabbi over from Cleveland once a year. Otherwise it's Dr. Donehower and other great Ohio thinkers. The rabbi's passionate devotion to the concept of kindness was enough to cure me of chapel for good."

"How much do you have to pay?"

"For a proxy? Two bucks a pop. It's nothing."

"Forty times two is eighty dollars. That's not nothing."

"Look," he said, "figure you spend fifteen minutes getting down off the Hill and over to the church. And if you're you, serious you, you don't laugh off being there. You don't laugh off anything. Instead you spend an hour at chapel seething with rage. Then you spend another fifteen minutes seething with rage while getting back up the Hill to wherever you're going next. That's ninety minutes. Ninety times forty equals sixty hours of rage. That's not nothing either."

"How do you find the person to pay? Explain to me how it works."

"The person you hire takes the card the usher hands him at the door when he goes in, then he hands it back signed with your name when he goes out. That's it. You think a handwriting specialist pores over each card back in the little office where they keep the records? They tick off your name in some ledger, and that's it. In the old days they used to assign you a seat and have a proctor who got to know everyone's face walk up and down the aisles to see who was missing. Back then you were screwed. But after the war they changed it, so now all you have to do is pay someone to take your place."

"But who?"

"Anyone. Anyone who's done his forty chapels. It's work. You work waiting tables at the taproom of the inn, someone else works proxying at the Methodist church. I'll find you somebody if you want me to. I can even try to find somebody for less than two bucks."

"And if this person shoots off his mouth? Then you're out of here on your ass."

"I've never heard yet of anybody shooting off his mouth. It's a business, Marcus. You make a simple business arrangement."

"But surely Caudwell knows this is going on."

"Caudwell's the biggest Christer around. He can't imagine why students don't *love* listening to Dr. Donehower instead of having the hour free every Wednesday to jack off in their rooms. Oh, that was a big mistake you made, bringing up chapel with Caudwell. Hawes D. Caudwell is the idol of this place. Winesburg's greatest halfback in football, greatest slugger in baseball, greatest center in basketball, greatest exponent on the planet of 'the Winesburg tradition.' Meet this guy head-on about upholding the Winesburg tradition and he'll make you into mush. Remember the drop kick, the old vintage drop kick? Caudwell holds the Winesburg record for drop-kicking points in a single season. And you know what he called each of those drop kicks? 'A drop kick for Christ.' You go around such creeps, Marcus. A little detachment goes a long way at Winesburg. Keep your mouth shut, your ass covered, smile—and then do whatever you like. Don't take it all personally, don't take everything so seriously, and you might find this is not the worst place in the world to spend the best years of your life. You already located the Blowjob Queen of 1951. That's a start."

"I don't know what you're talking about."

"You mean she *didn't* blow you? You *are* unique."

Angrily, I said, "I still don't know what you're referring to."

"To Olivia Hutton."

Fury swiftly mounted in me, the very fury that I'd felt toward Elwyn when he called Olivia a cunt. "Now why do you say that about Olivia Hutton?"

"Because blowjobs are at a premium in north-central Ohio. News of Olivia has traveled fast. Don't look so puzzled."

"I don't believe this."

"You should. Miss Hutton is a bit of a nutcase."

"Now why do you say *that?* I took her out."

"So did I."

That stunned me. I jumped up from the bench and, in a dizzying state of confusion about what there was (or wasn't) in me that made relations with others so wretchedly disappointing, fled Sonny Cottler and sped off to my government class, and the last words of his I heard were "Withdraw 'nutcase.' Okay? Let's say she's the kind of oddball who's exceptionally good at sex, and it's a function of being disturbed—all right? Marcus? Marc?"

The vomiting resumed that night, accompanied by stabbing stomach pain and diarrhea, and when finally I realized I was ill because of something other than my interview with Dean Caudwell, I made my way through the dawn light to the Student Health Office, where before I could even be interviewed by the on-duty nurse, I had to make a run for the toilet. I was then given a cot to lie down on, at seven I was examined by the college doctor, by eight I was in an ambulance bound for the community hospital twenty-five miles away, and by noon my appendix had been removed.

My first visitor was Olivia. She came the next day, having learned of my operation in history class the previous afternoon. She rapped on the half-open door to my room, arriving only seconds after I had got off the telephone with my parents, who had been contacted by Dean Caudwell after it was determined at the hospital that I needed emergency surgery. "Thank God you had the sense to go to the doctor," my father said, "and they caught it in time. Thank God nothing terrible happened." "Dad, it was my appendix. They took out my appendix. That's all that happened." "But suppose they hadn't diagnosed it." "But they *did*. Everything went perfectly. I'll be out of the hospital in four or five days." "You had an emergency appendectomy. You understand what an emergency is?" "But the emergency's *over*. There's no need for any more worrying." "There's plenty of need for worrying when it comes to you."

Here my father had to pause because of his hacking cough. It sounded worse than ever. When he was able to resume speaking, he asked, "Why are they letting you out so soon?" "Four or five days is normal. There's no need for me to be hospitalized longer." "I'm going to take the train out there after they discharge you. I'm shutting the store and I'm coming out there." "Don't, Dad. Don't talk that way. I appreciate the offer, but I'll be fine in the dorm." "Who will look after you in the dorm? You should recuperate in your house, where you belong. I don't understand why the college doesn't insist on this. How can you recuperate away from your home with nobody looking after you?" "But I'm up and walking already. I'm fine already." "How far is the hospital from the college?" I was tempted to say "Seventeen thousand miles," but he was coughing too painfully for me to be satirizing him. "Less than half an hour by ambulance," I said. "It's an excellent hospital." "There's no hospital there in Winesburg itself? Am I understanding you correctly?" "Dad, put Mother on. This isn't helping me any. And it isn't helping you. You sound awful." "I sound awful? You're the one in a hospital hundreds of miles away from home." "Please let me talk to Mother." When my mother came on, I told her to do something to contain him or next I'd transfer to the University of the North Pole, where there were no phones, hospitals, or doctors, just polar bears who stalk the ice floes where the undergraduates, naked in subzero temperatures— "Marcus, that's enough. I'm coming to see you." "But you don't have to come—neither of you has to come. It was an easy operation, it's over, and I'm fine." Whispering, she said, "*I* know that. But your father will not let up. I'm leaving here on the Saturday night train. Otherwise nobody in this house will sleep ever again."

Olivia. I hung up from speaking to my mother and there she was. In her arms she had a bouquet of flowers. She carried them over to where I lay propped up in the bed.

"It's no fun being in a hospital alone," she said. "I brought these to keep you company."

"It was worth the appendicitis," I replied.

"I doubt it," she said. "Were you very ill?"

"For less than a day. The best part came in Dean Caudwell's office. He called me in to grill me about changing my dorm room and I puked on his trophies. Then you turn up. It's been a great case of appendicitis all around."

"Let me get a vase for these."

"What are they?"

"You don't know?" she said, holding the bouquet to my nose.

"I know concrete. I know asphalt. I don't know flowers."

"They're called roses, dear."

When she came back into the room, she'd taken the roses out of their paper wrapping and arranged them in a glass vase half filled with water.

"Where will you be able to see them best?" she asked me, looking around the room, which, though small, was still larger and certainly brighter than the one I occupied in Neil Hall. At Neil Hall there was only a small dormer window up in the eaves, while here two good-sized windows looked out onto a well-tended lawn where somebody was trailing a rake along the ground, gathering the fallen leaves into a heap to burn. It was Friday, October 26, 1951. The Korean War was one year, four months, and one day old.

"I see them best," I said, "in your two hands. I see them best with you standing there. Just stay like that and let me look at you and your roses. That's what I came for." Yet by saying "hands," I caused myself to remember what Sonny Cottler had said about her, and again the fury rose in me, directed at both Cottler *and* Olivia. But so too did my penis rise.

"What are they giving you to eat?" she asked.

"Jell-O and ginger ale. Tomorrow they begin with the snails."

"You seem very chipper."

She was so beautiful! How could she blow Sonny Cottler? But then how could she blow me? If he took her out only once, then she would have blown him on the first date too. Too, the torment of that "too"!

"Look," I said, and pulled back the sheets.

Demurely, she lowered her lashes. "What happens, my master, should someone walk in?"

I couldn't believe that's what she had said, but then I couldn't believe what I had just done. Was it she who emboldened me, or I who emboldened her, or we two who emboldened each other?

"Is the wound draining?" she asked. "Is that tube dangling down there a drain?"

"I don't know. I can't tell. I suppose so."

"What about stitches?"

"This is a hospital. Where better to be when they come undone?"

There was a gently erotic sway to her gait as she slowly approached the bed pointing a finger at my erection. "You are odd, you know. Very odd," she told me, once she'd at last arrived at my side. "Odder than I think you realize."

"I'm always odd after I have my appendix out."

"Do you always get as huge as this after you've had your appendix out?"

"Never fails." Huge. She'd said huge. *Was* it?

"Of course we shouldn't," she whispered mischievously while wrapping my dick in her hand. "We could both get thrown out of school for this."

"Then stop!" I whispered back, realizing that, of course, she was right—that's exactly what would happen: caught and thrown out of school, she to slouch back home in shame to Hunting Valley, I to be drafted and killed.

But then she hadn't to stop, she hadn't even really to begin, because I had already ejaculated high in the air, and down over the bedsheets the semen showered, while Olivia recited sweetly, "I shot an arrow into the air / It fell to earth I knew not where" and just as my nurse walked through the door to take my temperature.

She was a round, gray-haired, middle-aged spinster named Miss Clement, the epitome of the thoughtful, soft-spoken, old-fashioned nurse—she even wore a starched white bonnet, unlike most of the younger nurses on the hospital staff. When I'd had to use the bedpan for the first time after the surgery, she'd quietly reassured me, saying, "I'm here to help you while you need help, and this is the help you now need, and there's nothing to be embarrassed about," and all the while she was gently positioning me over the bedpan and then cleaning me with moist toilet tissue and finally removing the pan containing my slime and settling me back under the sheets.

And this was her reward for ever so tenderly wiping my ass. And mine? For that one quick stroke of Olivia's hand, my reward would be Korea. Miss Clement must already be on the phone to Dean Caudwell, who'd himself be on the phone to my father following that. And easily enough I could envision my father, after receiving the news, swinging the meat cleaver with such force as to split wide open the four-foot-thick freestanding butcher block on which he ordinarily cracked open the carcasses of cows.

"Excuse me," murmured Miss Clement and, pulling the door closed, disappeared. Quickly Olivia went into my bathroom and returned with hand towels, one for the bed linens, another for me.

Struggling to feign a manly calm, I asked Olivia, "What's she going to do now? What's going to happen next?"

"Nothing," Olivia replied.

"You're awfully poised about this. Is it all the practice you've had?"

Her voice was husky when she replied. "It wasn't necessary to say that."

"I apologize. I'm sorry. But this is all new to me."

"You don't think it's new to *me?*"

"What about Sonny Cottler?"

"I don't see where that's your business," she shot back.

"Isn't it?"

"*No.*"

"You're awfully poised about *everything*," I said. "How do you know the nurse is going to do nothing?"

"She's too embarrassed to."

"Look, how did you get like this?"

"Like what?" asked Olivia, in anger now.

"So—expert."

"Oh, yes, Olivia the expert," she said sourly. "That's what they called me at the Menninger Clinic."

"But you are. You're so under control."

"You really think so, do you? I, who have eight thousand moods a minute, whose every emotion is a tornado, who can be thrown by a *word*, by a *syllable*, am 'under control'? God, you *are* blind," she said and went back to the bathroom with the towels.

Olivia came by bus to the hospital the next day— a fifty-minute bus ride in either direction—and in my room the same delightful business transpired, after which she cleaned up and, while in the bathroom disposing of the towels, changed the water in the vase to keep the flowers fresh.

Miss Clement now tended to me without speaking. Despite Olivia's reassurance, I couldn't believe that she hadn't told someone, and that the payoff would come when I left the hospital and was back at school. I was as sure as my own father would have been that as a result of my having been caught having sexual contact with Olivia in my hospital room, full-scale disaster would shortly ensue.

Olivia was fascinated by my being a butcher's son. It seemed far more interesting to her that I should be a butcher's son than what was of no little interest to me, that she should be a doctor's daughter. I'd never before dated a doctor's daughter. Mostly the girls I'd known were girls whose fathers owned a neighborhood store, like my father did, or were salesmen who sold neckties or aluminum siding or life insurance, or were tradesmen—electricians, plumbers, and so forth. At the hospital, after I'd had my orgasm, she almost immediately began asking me about the store, and very quickly I got the idea: I was to her something on the order of the child of a snake charmer or of a circus performer raised in the big top. "Tell me more," she said. "I want to hear more." "Why?" I asked. "Because I know nothing about such things and because I like you so much. I want to learn everything about you. I want to know what made you you, Marcus."

"Well, the store made me me, if anything did, though what exactly was made I can't say I entirely know anymore. I've been in a very confused state of mind since I hit this place."

"It made you hardworking. It made you honest. It gave you integrity."

"Oh, did it?" I said. "The butcher shop?"

"Absolutely."

"Well, let me tell you about the fat man, then," I said. "Let me tell you what he gave me in the way of integrity. We'll start with him."

"Goodie. Story time. The fat man and how he gave Marcus integrity." She laughed in anticipation. The laugh of a child being tickled. Nothing exceptional, and still it enchanted me as much as everything else.

"Well, a fat man used to come every Friday and pick up all the fat. It's possible he had a name, though it's equally possible that he didn't. He was just the fat man. He would come in once a week, announce, 'Fat man here,' weigh all the fat, pay my father for it, and take it away. The fat was in a garbage pail, a regular fifty-five-gallon pail about this high, and while we were cutting we were tossing the fat into the pail there. Before the big Jewish holidays, when people loaded up with meat, there could be a couple of pailfuls waiting for him. It couldn't have been a lot of money that the fat man paid. A couple of bucks a week, no more than that. Well, our store was right near the corner where the bus to downtown stopped, the number eight Lyons Avenue bus. And on Fridays, after the fat man picked up the fat, he left behind the garbage cans, and I had the job of washing them out. I remember once one of the pretty girls from my class saying to me, 'Oh, when I stopped at the bus stop in front of your father's store, I saw you there cleaning out the garbage cans.' So I went to my father and said, 'This is ruining my social life. I can't clean these garbage cans anymore.'"

"You cleaned them in front of the store?" Olivia asked. "Right out on the street?"

"Where else?" I said. "I had a scrub brush, Ajax, threw a little water in with the Ajax, and I'd scrub the inside of it. If you didn't get it clean, it would start to smell. Become rancid. But you don't want to hear this stuff."

"I do. I do."

"I had you down for a great woman of the world, but in many ways you're a child, aren't you?"

"But of course. Isn't it a triumph at my age? Would you have it any other way? Continue. Washing the garbage cans after the fat man left."

"Well, you'd get a pail of water, pour it in, swish it around, and empty it into the gutter, and from there it would flow down along the curbstone, carrying with it all the street-side debris, and then drain into the sewer grate at the corner. Then you'd do the whole thing a second time, and that would get the can clean."

"And so," said Olivia, laughing—no, not laughing, nibbling rather at the bait of a laugh—"you figured you weren't going to pick up a lot of girls like that."

"No, I wasn't. That's why I said to the boss—I always referred to my father as the boss in the store—I said, 'Boss, I cannot do these garbage cans anymore. These girls from school are coming by, they stop in front of the store because of the bus, they see me cleaning garbage cans, and the next day I'm supposed to ask them to go out to a Saturday night movie with me? Boss, I can't do it.' And he said to me, 'You're ashamed? Why? What are you ashamed of? The only thing you have to be ashamed of is stealing. Nothing else. You clean the garbage cans.'"

"How terrific," she said, and captivated me now with a different laugh entirely, a laugh that was laden with the love of life for all its unexpected charms. At that moment you would have thought the whole of Olivia lay in her laughter, when in fact it lay in her scar.

It was also "terrific" and amused her greatly when I told her about Big Mendelson, who worked for my father when I was a little kid. "Big Mendelson had a nasty mouth on him," I said. "He really belonged in the back, in the refrigerator, and not in front waiting on customers. But I was seven or eight, and because he had this nasty kind of humor and because they called him Big Mendelson, I thought he was the funniest man on earth. Finally my father had to get rid of him."

"What did Big Mendelson do that he had to get rid of him?"

"Well, on Thursday mornings," I told her, "my

father would come back from the chicken market and he would dump all the chickens in a pile and people would pick whatever chicken they wanted for the weekend. Dumped them on a table. Anyway, one woman, a Mrs. Sklon, she used to pick up a chicken and smell the mouth and then smell the rear end. Then she'd pick up another chicken, and again she'd smell the mouth and then smell the rear end. She did the same thing every week, and she did it so many times every week that Big Mendelson couldn't contain himself, and one day he said, 'Mrs. Sklon, can *you* pass that inspection?' She got so mad at him, she picked up a knife from the counter and said, 'If you ever talk to me that way again, I'll stab you.'"

"And that's why your father let him go?"

"Had to. By then he'd said lots of things like that. But about Mrs. Sklon Big Mendelson was right. Mrs. Sklon was no picnic even for me, and I was the nicest boy in the world."

"I never doubted that," Olivia said.

"Well, for good or bad, that's what I was."

"Am. Are."

"Mrs. Sklon was the only one of the customers who didn't want to fix me up with their daughters.

I couldn't trick Mrs. Sklon," I said. "No one could. I would deliver to her. And every time I delivered she would take the order apart. And it was always a big order. And she would take it out of the bag and undo the wax paper and take everything out and weigh everything to make sure the weight was correct. I had to stand there and watch this show. I was always in a rush because I was always looking to deliver the orders as fast as I could and then get back to the schoolyard to play ball. So at a certain point I'd bring her order around to the back door, plop it down on the top step, knock on the door once, and run like hell. And she would catch me. Every time. 'Messner! Marcus Messner! The butcher's son! Come back here!' I always felt, when I was with Mrs. Sklon, that I was at the heart of things. I felt that with Big Mendelson. I mean what I'm saying, Olivia. I felt that with people in the butcher shop. I got enjoyment out of that butcher shop." But only before, I thought, before his thoughts made my father defenseless.

"And she had a scale in the kitchen, Mrs. Sklon—was that it?" Olivia asked me.

"In the kitchen, yes. But it was not an accurate scale. It was a baby scale. Besides, she never found that there was anything wrong. But she always weighed the meat, and she always caught me when I tried to run away. I could never escape this woman. She used to give me a quarter tip. A quarter was a good tip. Most were nickels and dimes."

"You had humble origins. Like Abe Lincoln. Honest Marcus."

"Insatiate Olivia."

"What about the war, when meat was rationed? What about the black market? Was your father in the black market?"

"Did he bribe the owner of the slaughterhouse? He did. But his customers didn't have ration stamps sometimes, and they were having company, they were having family over, and he wanted them to have meat, so he would give the slaughterhouse owner some cash each week, and he was able to get more meat. It wasn't a big deal. It was as easy as that. But otherwise my father was a man who never broke the law. I think that was the only law he ever broke in his life, and in those days everyone broke that one, more or less. You know kosher meat has to be washed every three days. My father would take a whisk broom with a bucket of water and wash all the meat down. But sometimes you had a Jewish holiday, and though we ourselves weren't strictly observant, we were Jews in a Jewish neighborhood, and what's more, kosher butchers, and so the store was closed. And one Jewish holiday, my father told me, he forgot. Say the Passover Seder was going to be on a Monday and a Tuesday, and he washed the meat on the previous Friday. He would have to come back on Monday or Tuesday to do it again, and this one time he forgot. Well, nobody knew he'd forgotten, but he knew, and he would not sell that meat to anyone. He took it all and sold it at a loss to Mueller, who had a nonkosher butcher store on Bergen Street. Sid Mueller. But he would not sell it to his customers. He took the loss instead."

"So you did learn to be honest from him in the store."

"Probably. I certainly can't say I ever learned anything bad from him. That would have been impossible."

"Lucky Marcus."

"You think so?"

"I know so," Olivia said.

"Tell me about being a doctor's daughter."

All color passed out of her face when she replied, "There's nothing to tell."

"You—"

She let me get no further. "Practice *tact*," she said coldly, and with that, as though a switch had been thrown or a plug pulled—as though gloom had swept through her like a storm—her face simply shut down. For the first time in my presence, so too did the beauty. Gone. The play and the luster suddenly gone, the fun of the butcher shop stories gone, and replaced by a terrible, sick-looking pallor the instant I wanted to know more about her.

I feigned indifference but I was shocked, so shocked that I blotted out the moment almost immediately. It was as if I'd been spun round and round till I was giddy and needed first to regain my balance, before I could reply, "Tact it is, then, and tact it shall be." But I wasn't happy, and earlier I'd been *so* happy, not just because of my raising Olivia's laughter but because of my remembering my father as he'd once been—as he'd always been —back in those unimperiled, unchanging days when everybody felt safe and settled in his place. I'd been remembering my father as if that's the way he still was and our lives had never taken this freakish turn. I'd been remembering him when he was anything but defenseless—when he was, without dispute, untyrannically, reassuringly, matter-of-factly boss, and I, his child and beneficiary, had felt so astonishingly free.

Why wouldn't she answer me when I asked what it was like to be a doctor's daughter? At first I blotted out that moment, but later it returned and wouldn't go away. Was it the divorce she didn't want to talk about? Or was it something worse? "Practice tact." Why? What did that mean?

On Sunday, in the late morning, my mother arrived and we went to speak alone together in the solarium at the end of the corridor. I wanted to show her how steady I was on my feet and how far I could walk and how well I felt altogether. I was thrilled to see her here, away from New Jersey, in a part of the country unknown to her—nothing like that had ever happened before—but knew that when Olivia came I would have to introduce the two of them and that my mother, who missed nothing, would see the scar on Olivia's wrist and ask me what I was doing with a girl who had tried to commit suicide, a question whose answer I didn't yet know. Rarely an hour went by when I didn't ask it of myself.

I thought at first to tell Olivia not to visit on the day that my mother was coming. But I'd already hurt her enough by stupidly alluding to her blowing Cottler and then again when I'd asked in all innocence for her to tell me about being a doctor's daughter. I didn't want to hurt her again, and so did nothing to keep her slashed wrist out of the range of my hawk-eyed mother. I did nothing—which is to say, I did exactly the wrong thing. Again.

My mother was exhausted from her overnight train journey—followed by an hourlong bus ride— and though it was only a couple of months since I'd seen her at home, she struck me as a much older, more haggard mother than the one I'd left behind. A harried look I was unaccustomed to seeing deepened her wrinkles and pervaded her features and seemed ingrained in her very skin. Though I kept reassuring her about me—and trying to reassure myself about her—and though I lied about how happy I was with everything at Winesburg, she emanated a sadness so uncharacteristic of her that finally I had to ask, "Ma, is there something wrong that I don't know?"

"Something's wrong that you do know. Your father," she said and startled me further by beginning to cry. "Something is very wrong with your father, and I don't know what it is."

"Is he sick? Does he have something?"

"Markie, I think he's losing his mind. I don't know what else to call it. You know how he was with you on the phone about the operation? That's how he is now about everything. Your father, who could confront any hardship in the family, survive any ordeal with the store, be pleasant to the worst of the customers—even after we were robbed that time and the thieves locked him in the refrigerator and emptied the register, you remember how he said, 'The money we can replace. Thank God nothing happened to any of us.' The same man who could say that, and *believe* that, now he can't do anything without a million worries. This is the man who when Abe got killed in the war held Uncle Muzzy and Aunt Hilda together, who when Dave got killed in the war held Uncle Shecky and Aunt Gertie together, who to this day has held together the whole Messner family, with all of their tragedies —and now you should see what happens when all he's doing is driving the truck. He's been driving around Essex County all his life and now suddenly he's delivering orders as though everyone on the road is a maniac except him. 'Look at the guy—look what he did. Did you see that woman—is she crazy? Why must people cross with the yellow light? Do they want to get run down, do they not want to live to see their grandchildren grow up and go to school and get married?' I serve him his dinner and he sniffs at his food as if I'm trying to poison him. This is true. 'Is this fresh?' he says. 'Smell this.' Food prepared by me in my own spotless kitchen and he won't eat it for fear that it's spoiled and will poison him. We're at the table, just the two of us, and I'm eating and he's not. It's horrible. He sits there not taking a bite and waiting to see if I keel over."

"And is he like that at the store?"

"Yes. Fearful all the time. 'We're losing customers. The supermarket is ruining our business. They're selling choice for prime, don't think I don't know it. They don't give customers an honest weight, they're charging them seventeen cents a pound for chicken, and then they turn around and get it up to twenty on the scale. I know how they work it, I know for a fact that they're cheating the customer—' On it goes, darling, night and day. It is true that our business is off, but everybody's business is off in Newark. People are moving to the suburbs and the businesses are following behind. The neighborhood is undergoing a revolution. Newark's not the same as it was during the war. Many people in the city are hurting suddenly, but still, it isn't as though we're starving to death. We have expenses to meet, but who doesn't? Do I complain about working again? No. Never. Yet that's how he acts. I prepare and wrap an order the same way I've been preparing and wrapping orders for twenty-five years, and he tells me, 'Not like that— the customers don't like it like that! You're in such a hurry to go home, look how you wrap it!' He even complains how I take orders on the phone. The customers always love to talk to me, to give the orders to me, because I show some concern. Now I talk too much to the customers. He has no patience anymore for me to be nice to our customers! I'm on the phone taking an order, and I say, 'Oh, so your grandchildren are going to be coming. That's nice. How do they like school?' And your father will pick up the other phone and tell the customer, 'You want to talk to my wife, you call at night, not during business hours,' and he hangs up. If this goes on, if he keeps this up, if I have to keep watching him push the peas around the plate with his fork, looking like a crazy man for the cyanide pill . . . Darling, is this what they call a personality change or has something terrible happened to him? Is it something new—is that possible? Out of nowhere? At fifty? Or is it something long buried that has come to the surface? Have I been living all these years with a time bomb? All I know is that something has made my husband into a different person. My own dear husband, and now I am completely confused about whether he is one man or two!"

She ended there, in tears again, the mother who never cried, never faltered, a well-spoken American-born girl who picked up Yiddish from him so as to speak it to the elderly customers, a South Side High graduate who'd taken the commercial course there and could have easily worked as a bookkeeper at a desk in an office but who learned to butcher and prepare meat from him in order to work beside him in the store instead, whose bedrock dependability, whose sensible words and coherent thoughts, had filled me with confidence throughout a childhood that was unembattled. And she became a bookkeeper in the end anyway—a bookkeeper *also*, I should say, who after coming home from working all day at the store kept the accounts at night and spent the last day of each month sending out the bills on our own lined "Messner Kosher Meat" billing stationery with the little drawing of a cow on the upper left side and the drawing of a chicken on the upper right. When I was a child, what could buoy me up more than the sight of those drawings at the top of our billing stationery and the fortitude of the two of them? Once upon a time an admirable, well-organized, hardworking family, emanating unity, and now he was frightened of everything and she was out of her mind with grief over what she wasn't entirely sure whether or not to label a "personality change"—and I had as good as run away from home.

"Maybe you should have told me," I said. "Why didn't you tell me it was so extensive?"

"I didn't want to bother you at school. You had your studies."

"But when do you think this began?"

"The first night he locked you out of the house, that's when. That night changed everything. You don't know how I fought with him before you got home that night. I never told you. I didn't want to embarrass him further. 'What are you accomplishing by double-locking the door?' I asked him. 'Do you really want your son not to come into the house, is that why you're double-locking it? You think you're teaching him a lesson,' I told him. 'What will you do if he teaches *you* a lesson and goes somewhere else to sleep? Because that's what a person with any sense does when he finds himself locked out—he doesn't stand around in the cold, waiting to get pneumonia. He gets up and he goes where it's warm and he's welcome. He'll go to a friend, you'll see. He'll go to Stanley's house. He'll go to Alan's house. And their parents will let him in. He won't take this sitting down, not Markie.' But your father refused to budge. 'How do I know where he is at this hour? How do I know he's not in some whorehouse?' We're lying in bed and that's what he's hollering—about whether my son is in a whorehouse or not. 'How do I know,' he asks me, 'that he's not out at this hour ruining his life?' I couldn't control him, and this is the result."

"What is the result?"

"You are now living in the middle of Ohio and he's running around the house shouting, 'Why is he having his appendix out in a hospital five hundred miles from home? There aren't hospitals in New Jersey to take out an appendix? The best hospitals in the world are right here in this state! What is he doing out there in the first place?' Fear, Marcus, fear leaking out at every pore, anger leaking out at every pore, and I don't know how to stop either one."

"Take him to a doctor, Mom. Take him to one of those wonderful hospitals in New Jersey and get them to find out what is wrong with him. Maybe they can give him something to settle him down."

"Don't make fun of this, Markie. Don't make fun of your father. This has all the earmarks of a tragedy."

"But I *meant* it. It sounds like he should see a doctor. See *somebody*. It all can't fall on you like this."

"But your father is your father. He won't take an aspirin for a headache. He won't give in. He won't even go to see the doctor about the cough. People coddle themselves, in his eyes. 'It's smoking,' he says, and saying that settles it. 'My father smoked all his life. I've been smoking all my life. Shecky, Muzzy, and Artie have smoked all their lives. Messners smoke. I don't need a doctor to tell me how to cut a shoulder steak, and I don't need a doctor to tell me about smoking.' He can't drive in traffic now without blowing his horn at everybody who comes anywhere near him, and when I tell him there's no need for the horn, he shouts, 'There *isn't?* With madmen out driving cars on the roads?' But it's him—he's the madman on the roads. And I can't take anymore."

Concerned as I was for my mother's well-being, disturbed as I was to see her so shaken—she who was the anchor and the mainstay of our home, who, behind the counter of the butcher shop, was every bit the artist with a meat cleaver that he was—I remembered from listening to her why I was at Winesburg. Forget chapel, forget Caudwell, forget Dr. Donehower's sermons and the girls' convent curfew hours and everything else wrong with this place—endure what is and make it work. Because by leaving home you saved your life. You saved his. Because I would have shot him to shut him up. I could shoot him now for what he was doing to her. Yet what he was doing to himself was worse. And how do you shoot someone whose onset of craziness at the age of fifty wasn't just disrupting his wife's life and irreparably altering his son's life but devastating his own?

"Mom, you've got to get him to Dr. Shildkret. He trusts Dr. Shildkret. He swears by Dr. Shild-kret. Let's hear what Dr. Shildkret thinks." I did not myself have a high regard for Shildkret, least of all for his thinking; he was our doctor only because he'd gone to grade school with my father and grown up penniless on the same Newark slum street. Because Shildkret's father was "a lazy bas-tard" and his mother a long-suffering woman who, in my father's kindly estimation, qualified as "a saint," their moron of a son was our family doctor. Woe unto us, but I didn't know who or what else to recommend other than Shildkret.

"He won't go," my mother said. "I already sug-gested it. He refuses to go. There's nothing wrong with him—it's the rest of the world that's in the wrong."

"Then *you* see Shildkret. Tell him what's happen-ing. Hear what he says. Maybe he can send him to a specialist."

"A specialist in driving around Newark without honking the horn at every car nearby? No. I could not do that to your father."

"Do what?"

"Embarrass him like that in front of Dr. Shild-kret. If he knew I went and talked about this behind his back, it would crush him."

"So instead he crushes you? Look at you. You're a wreck. You, as strong as a person can be, and you have become a wreck. The kind of wreck I would have become had I stayed with him in that house another day."

"Darling"—here she grasped at my hand—"dar-ling, should I? Can I possibly? I came all this way to ask you. You're the only one I can talk to about this."

"Could you possibly what? What are you asking?"

"I can't say the word."

"What word?" I asked.

"Divorce." And then, my hand still in hers, she used both of our hands together to cover her mouth. Divorce was unknown in our Jewish neigh-borhood. I was led to believe it was all but unknown in the Jewish world. Divorce was shameful. Divorce was scandalous. Breaking up a family with a divorce was virtually a criminal act. Growing up, I'd never known of a single household among my friends or my schoolmates or our family's friends where the parents were divorced or were drunks or, for that matter, owned a dog. I was raised to think all three repugnant. My mother could have stunned me more only if she'd told me she'd gone out and bought a Great Dane.

"Oh, Ma, you're trembling. You're in a state of shock." As was I. *Would* she? Why not? I'd run off to Winesburg—why shouldn't she get a divorce? "You've been married to him for twenty-five years. You love him."

Vigorously, she shook her head. "I don't! I hate him! I sit in the car while he's driving and screaming to me about how everybody is in the wrong except him, and I hate and I loathe him from the bottom of my heart!"

By such vehemence we were both astonished. "That is not true," I said. "Even if it seems true now, it's not a permanent condition. It's only because I'm gone and you're all on your own with him and you don't know what to do with him. Please go see Dr. Shildkret. At least as a start. Ask his advice." Meanwhile, I was afraid of Shildkret's saying, "He's right. People don't know how to drive anymore. I've noticed this myself. You get into your car these days, you take your life into your hands."

Shildkret was a dope and a lousy doctor, and it was my good luck that I had come down with appendicitis nowhere in his vicinity. He would have prescribed an enema and killed me.

Killed me. I'd caught it from my father. All I could think about were the ways I could be killed. *You are odd, you know. Very odd. Odder than I think you realize.* And Olivia should know how to spot oddness, should she not?

"I'm seeing a lawyer," my mother then told me.

"No."

"Yes. I've already seen him. I have an attorney," she said, the helpless way one would say, "I've gone bankrupt" or "I'm going in for a lobotomy." "I went on my own," she said. "I can't live any longer with your father in that house. I cannot work with him in the store. I cannot drive with him in the car. I cannot sleep beside him in the bed anymore. I don't want him near me like that—he's too angry a person to lie next to. It frightens me. That's what I came to tell you." Now she was no longer crying. Now suddenly she was herself, ready and able to do battle, and I was the one at the edge of tears, knowing that none of this would be happening had I remained at home.

It takes muscle to be a butcher, and my mother had muscles, and I felt them when she took me in her arms while I cried.

When we walked from the solarium back to the room—passing on the way Miss Clement, who, like the saint *she* was, kindly kept her gaze averted—Olivia was there arranging a second bouquet of flowers she'd brought with her on her arrival a few minutes earlier. Her sweater sleeves were pushed up so as not to get them wet with the water she'd put into a second vase she'd found, and so there was her scar, the scar on the wrist of the very hand with which she had driven Miss Clement into silence, the very hand with which we pursued our indecent ends in a hospital room while around us in the other rooms people were behaving according to rules that didn't even allow for loud talking. Now Olivia's scar looked to me as prominent as if she had cut herself open only days before.

As a child, I had sometimes been taken by my father to the slaughterhouse on Astor Street in Newark's Ironbound section. And I had been taken to the chicken market at the far end of Bergen

Street. At the chicken market I saw them killing the chickens. I saw them kill hundreds of chickens according to the kosher laws. First my father would pick out the chickens he wanted. They were in a cage, maybe five tiers high, and he would reach in to pull one out, hold on to its head so it didn't bite him, and feel the sternum. If it wiggled, the chicken was young and was not going to be tough; if it was rigid, more than likely the chicken was old and tough. He would also blow on its feathers so he could see the skin—he wanted the flesh to be yellow, a little fatty. Whichever ones he picked, he put into one of the boxes that they had, and then the *shochet*, the slaughterer, would ritually slaughter them. He would bend the neck backward—not break it, just arc it back, maybe pull a few of the feathers to get the neck clear so he could see what he was doing—and then with his razor-sharp knife he would cut the throat. For the chicken to be kosher he had to cut the throat in one smooth, deadly stroke. One of the strangest sights I remember from my early youth was the slaughtering of the nonkosher chickens, where they lopped the head right off. Swish! Plop! Whereupon they put the headless chicken down into a funnel. They had about six or seven funnels in a circle. There the blood could drain from the body into a big barrel. Sometimes the chickens' legs were still moving, and occasionally a chicken would fall out of the funnel and, as the saying has it, begin running around with its head cut off. Such chickens might bump into a wall but they ran anyway. They put the kosher chickens in the funnels too. The bloodletting, the killing—my father was hardened to these things, but at the beginning I was of course unsettled, much as I tried not to show it. I was a little one, six, seven years old, but this was the business, and soon I accepted that the business was a mess. The same at the slaughterhouse, where to kosher the animal, you have to get the blood out. In a nonkosher slaughterhouse they can shoot the animal, they can knock it unconscious, they can kill it any way they want to kill it. But to be kosher they've got to bleed it to death. And in my days as a butcher's little son, learning what slaughtering was about, they would hang the animal by its foot to bleed it. First a chain is wrapped around the rear leg—they trap it that way. But that chain is also a hoist, and quickly they hoist it up, and it hangs from its heel so that all the blood will run down to the head and the upper body. Then they're ready to kill it. Enter *shochet* in skullcap. Sits in a little sort of alcove, at least at the Astor Street slaughterhouse he did, takes the head of the animal, lays it over his knees, takes a pretty big blade, says a *bracha*—a blessing—and he cuts the neck. If he does it in one slice, severs the trachea, the esophagus, and the carotids, and doesn't touch the backbone, the animal dies instantly and is kosher; if it takes two slices or the animal is sick or disabled or the knife isn't perfectly sharp or the backbone is merely nicked, the animal is not kosher. The *shochet* slits the throat from ear to ear and then lets the animal hang there until all the blood flows out. It's as if he took a bucket of blood, as if he took several buckets, and poured them out all at once, because that's how fast blood gushes from the arteries onto the floor, a concrete floor with a drain in it. He stands there in boots, in blood up to his ankles despite the drain—and I saw all this when I was a boy. I witnessed it many times. My father thought it was important for me to see it—the same man who now was afraid of everything for me and, for whatever reason, afraid for himself.

My point is this: that is what Olivia had tried to

do, to kill herself according to kosher specifications by emptying her body of blood. Had she been successful, had she expertly completed the job with a single perfect slice of the blade, she would have rendered herself kosher in accordance with rabbinical law. Olivia's telltale scar came from attempting to perform her own ritual slaughter.

It was from my mother that I got my height. She was a big, heavyset woman, only one inch under six feet, towering not just over my father but over every mother in the neighborhood. With her dark bushy eyebrows and coarse gray hair (and, at the store, with her coarse gray clothes beneath a bloody white apron), she embodied the role of the laborer as convincingly as any Soviet woman in the propaganda posters about America's overseas allies that hung in the halls of our grade school during the years of World War Two. Olivia was slender and fair, and even at five-seven or -eight seemed diminutive beside my mother, so when the woman who was used to working in a bloody white apron wielding long knives as sharp as swords and opening and shutting the heavy refrigerator door gave Olivia her hand to shake, I saw not only what Olivia must have looked like as a small child but also what little protection she had against confusion when it came at her full force. Her delicate hand wasn't just clasped like a baby lamb chop in the big, bearish paw of my mother; she herself was still in the grip of whatever had driven her, only a few years beyond childhood, first to drink and then to the edge of destruction. She was yielding and fragile to the marrow of her bones, a *wounded* small child, and I finally grasped that only because my mother, even under assault from my father and prepared to go so far as to divorce him, which would be tantamount to killing him—yes, I now saw him dead too—was anything but fragile and yielding. That my father could have gotten my mother to go on her own to see a lawyer about a divorce was a measure not of her weakness but of the crushing power of his inexplicable transformation, of his all at once having been turned inside out by unrelenting intimations of catastrophe.

My mother called Olivia "Miss Hutton" throughout the twenty minutes they were together with me in my hospital room. Otherwise her behavior was impeccable, as was Olivia's. She asked Olivia no embarrassing questions, did not pry into her background or into what her arranging my flowers might signify about our acquaintance—*she* practiced tact. I introduced Olivia as the fellow student who was bringing my homework out to me and who was carrying back with her the written assignments I completed in order to keep abreast of my classes. I didn't once catch her looking at Olivia's wrists, nor did she register suspicion or disapproval of her in any way. If my mother hadn't married my father, she could, without difficulty, have held down any number of jobs far more demanding of the skills of diplomacy and the functioning of intelligence than what was required for work in a butcher shop. Her formidable figure belied the finesse she could marshal when circumstances required an astuteness in the ways of life of which my father was ignorant.

Olivia, as I said, didn't let me down either. She did not even wince at finding herself repeatedly being called Miss Hutton, though I did, each time. What was the something about her that necessitated such formality? It couldn't be because she wasn't Jewish. Though my mother was a Newark

Jewish provincial of her class and time and background, she wasn't a stupid provincial, and she
knew very well that by his living in the heart of the
American Midwest in the middle of the twentieth
century, her son was more than likely going to seek
out the company of girls born into the predomi-
nant, ubiquitous, all but official American faith.
Was it Olivia's appearance that put her off then, the
look of privilege that she had, as though she'd
never known a single hardship? Was it the slender
young female body? Was my mother unprepared
for that supple physical delicacy crowned by the
auburn abundance of that hair? Why again and
again "Miss Hutton" to a mannerly girl of nineteen
who had done nothing as far as she knew except to
help her recuperating son while he was a postoper-
ative hospital patient? What had affronted her?
What had alarmed her? It couldn't have been the
flowers, though they didn't help. It could only be a
quick glimpse of the scar that had made unspeak-
able and unsayable Olivia's given name. It was the
scar *together* with the flowers.

The scar had taken possession of my mother, and
Olivia knew it, and so did I. We all knew it, which
made nearly unendurable listening to whatever

words were spoken about anything else. Olivia's having lasted in the room with my mother for twenty minutes was a heartbreaking feat of gallantry and strength.

As soon as Olivia had left to take the bus back to Winesburg, my mother went into my bathroom, not to wash up but to clean out the sink, the tub, and the toilet bowl with soap and paper towels.

"Ma, don't," I called in to her. "You just got off a train. Everything is clean enough."

"I'm here, it needs it, I'll do it," she said.

"It *doesn't* need it. They did it this morning first thing."

But she needed it more than the bathroom needed it. Work—certain people yearn for work, any work, harsh or unsavory as it may be, to drain the harshness from their lives and drive from their minds the killing thoughts. By the time she came out, she was my mother again, scrubbing and scouring having restored the womanly warmth she'd always had at her disposal to give me. I remembered that when I was a child in school, *Ma at work* would always come to my mind whenever I thought of my mother, *Ma at work*, but not because work was her burden. To me her maternal grandeur stemmed from her being no less a powerhouse of a butcher than my father.

"So tell me about your studies," she said, settling into the chair in the corner of the room while I propped myself up against the pillows in my bed. "Tell me about what you're learning here."

"American History to 1865. From the first settlements in Jamestown and Massachusetts Bay to the end of the Civil War."

"And you like that?"

"I like it, Mom, yes."

"What else do you study?"

"The Principles of American Government."

"What is that about?"

"How the government works. Its foundations. Its laws. The Constitution. The separation of powers. The three branches. I had civics in high school, but never the government stuff this thoroughly. It's a good course. We read documents. We read some of the famous Supreme Court cases."

"That's wonderful for you. That's right up your alley. And the teachers?"

"They're all right. They're not geniuses, but

they're good enough. They're not what's uppermost anyway. I've got the books to study, I've got the library to use—I've got everything a brain requires for an education."

"And you're happier away from home?"

"I'm better off, Ma," I said, and better off, I thought, because you're not.

"Read me something, darling. Read me something from one of your school books. I want to hear what you're learning."

I took the first volume of *The Growth of the American Republic* that Olivia had brought me from my room and, opening it at random, hit upon the beginning of a chapter I'd already studied, "Jefferson's Administration," subtitled "1. The 'Revolution of 1800.'" "'Thomas Jefferson,'" I began, "'ruminating years later on the events of a crowded lifetime, thought that his election to the Presidency marked as real a revolution as that of 1776. He had saved the country from monarchy and militarism, and brought it back to republican simplicity. But there never had been any danger of monarchy; it was John Adams who saved the country from militarism; and a little simplicity cannot be deemed revolutionary.'"

I read further: "'Fisher Ames predicted that, with a "Jacobin" President, America would be in for a real reign of terror. Yet the four years that followed were one of the most tranquil of the Republican Olympiads, marked not by radical reforms or popular tumults . . .'" And when I looked up, midway through that sentence, I saw that my mother had fallen half asleep in her chair. There was a smile on her face. Her son was reading aloud to her what he was studying in college. It was worth the train ride and the bus ride and maybe even the sight of Miss Hutton's scar. For the first time in months, she was happy.

To keep her that way, I kept going. "' . . . but by the peaceful acquisition of territory as large again as the United States. The election of 1800–1801 brought a change of men more than of measures, and a transfer of federal power from the latitude of Massachusetts to that of Virginia . . .'" Now she was fully asleep, but I did not stop. Madison. Monroe. J. Q. Adams. I'd read right on through to Harry Truman if that was what it took to ease the woes of my having left her behind alone with a husband now out of control.

She spent the night in a hotel not far from the hospital and came again to visit me the next morning, Monday, before she left by bus for the train to take her home. I was to leave the hospital myself after lunch that day. Sonny Cottler had phoned me the night before. He had only just heard about my appendectomy, and despite the unpleasantness of our last meeting out on the quad—to which neither of us alluded—he insisted on coming out in his car to drive me from the hospital back to school, where arrangements had already been made by Dean Caudwell's office for me to spend the next week sleeping in a bed in the small infirmary adjacent to the Student Health Office. I could rest there when I needed to during the day and resume attending all my classes other than gym. I should be ready after that to climb the three flights to my room at the top of Neil Hall. And a couple of weeks after that to return to my job at the inn.

That Monday morning my mother looked herself again, unbroken and unbreakable. After I'd finished assuring her about the helpful arrangements the college had made for my return, the first thing she said was "I won't divorce him, Marcus. I made up my mind. I'll bear him. I'll do all I can to help him, if anything *can* help him. If that's what you want from me, that's what I want too. You don't want divorced parents, and I don't want you to have divorced parents. I'm sorry now that I even allowed myself such thoughts. I'm sorry that I told them to you. The way that I did it, here at the hospital, with you just out of bed and starting to walk around on your own—that wasn't right. That wasn't fair. I apologize. I will stay with him, Marcus, through thick and thin."

I filled up with tears and immediately put my hand over my eyes as though I could either hide my tears that way or manage with my fingers to hold them back.

"You can cry, Markie. I've seen you cry before."

"I know you have. I know I can. I don't want to. I'm just very happy . . ." I had to stop for a while to find my voice and to recover from having been reduced by her words to being the tiny creature who is nothing but its need of perpetual nurture. "I'm just very happy to hear what you said. This behavior of his could be a temporary thing, you know. Things like this happen, don't they, when people hit a certain age?"

"I'm sure they do," she said soothingly.

"Thank you, Ma. This is a great relief to me. I could not imagine him living alone. With only the store and his work and nothing to come home to at night, on his own on the weekends . . . it was unimaginable."

"It is worse than unimaginable," she said, "so don't imagine it. But now I must ask for something in return. Because something is unimaginable to me. I never asked anything of you before. I never asked anything of you before because I never had to. Because you are perfect where sons are concerned. All you've ever wanted to be is a boy who does well. You have been the best son any mother could have. But I am going to ask you to have nothing more to do with Miss Hutton. Because for you to be with her is unimaginable to *me*. Markie, you are here to be a student and to study the Supreme Court and to study Thomas Jefferson and to prepare to go to law school. You are here so someday you will become a person in the community that other people look up to and that they come to for help. You are here so you don't have to be a Messner like your grandfather and your father and your cousins and work in a butcher shop for the rest of your life. You are not here to look for trouble with a girl who has taken a razor and slit her wrists."

"Wrist," I said. "She slit one wrist."

"One is enough. We have only two, and one is too much. Markie, I will stay with your father and in return I will ask you to give her up before you get in over your head and don't know how to get out. I want to make a deal. Will you make that deal with me?"

"Yes," I replied.

"That's my boy! That's my tall, wonderful boy! The world is full of young women who have not slit any wrists—who have slit *nothing*. They exist by the millions. Find one of *them*. She can be a Gentile, she can be anything. This is 1951. You don't live in the old world of my parents and their parents and their parents before them. Why should you? That old world is far, far away and everything in it long gone. All that is left is the kosher meat. That's enough. That suffices. It has to. Probably it should. All the rest can go. The three of us never lived like people in a ghetto, and we're not starting now. We are Americans. Date anyone you want, marry anyone you want, do whatever you want with whoever you choose—as long as she's never put a razor to herself in order to end her life. A girl so wounded as to do such a thing is not for you. To want to wipe out everything before your life has even begun—absolutely not! You have no business with such a person, you don't need such a person, no matter what kind of goddess she looks like and how many beautiful flowers she brings you. She is a beautiful young woman, there is no doubt about that. Obviously she is well brought up. Though maybe there is more to her upbringing than meets the eye. You never know about those things. You never know the truth of what goes on in people's houses. When the child goes wrong, look first to the family. Regardless, my heart goes out to her. I have nothing against her. I wish the girl luck. I pray, for her sake, that her life does not come to nothing. But you are my only son and my only child, and my responsibility is not to her but to you. You must sever the connection completely. You must look elsewhere for a girlfriend."

"I understand," I said.

"Do you? Or are you saying so to avoid a fight?"

"I'm not afraid of a fight, Mother. You know that."

"I know you are strong. You stood up to your father and he is no weakling. And you were right to stand up to him; between the two of us, I was proud of you for standing up to him. But I hope that doesn't mean that when I leave here, you will change your mind. You won't, will you, Markie? When you get back to school, when she comes to see you, when she begins to cry and you see her tears, you won't change your mind? This is a girl full of tears. You see that the moment you look at her. Inside she is all tears. Can you stand up to her tears, Marcus?"

"Yes."

"Can you stand up to hysterical screaming, if it should come to that? Can you stand up to desperate pleading? Can you look the other way when someone in pain begs and begs you for what she wants that you won't give her? Yes, to a father you could say, 'It's none of your business—leave me alone!' But do you have the kind of strength that *this* requires? Because you also have a conscience. A conscience that I'm proud that you have, but a conscience that can be your enemy. You have a conscience and you have compassion and you have sweetness in you too—so tell me, do you know how to do such things as may be required of you with this girl? Because other people's weakness can destroy you just as much as their strength can. Weak people are not harmless. Their weakness can *be* their strength. A person so unstable is a menace to you, Markie, and a trap."

"Mom, you don't have to go on. Stop right here. We have a deal."

Here she took me in those arms of hers, arms as strong as mine, if not stronger, and she said, "You are an emotional boy. Emotional like your father and all of his brothers. You are a Messner like all the Messners. Once your father was the sensible one, the reasonable one, the only one with a head on his shoulders. Now, for whatever reason, he's as crazy as the rest. The Messners aren't just a family of butchers. They're a family of shouters and a family of screamers and a family of putting their foot down and banging their heads against the wall, and now, out of the blue, your father is as bad as the rest of them. Don't you be. You be *greater* than your feelings. I don't demand this of you—*life* does. Otherwise you'll be washed away by feelings. You'll be washed out to sea and never seen again. Feelings can be life's biggest problem. Feelings can play the most terrible tricks. They played them on me when I came to you and said I was going to divorce your father. Now I have dealt with those feelings. Promise me you will deal the same with yours."

"I promise you. I will."

We kissed, and thinking in unison of my father, we were as though welded together by our desperate passion for a miracle to occur.

At the infirmary, I was shown to the narrow hospital bed—one of three in a smallish, bright room looking onto the campus woods—that would be mine for the next week. The nurse showed me how to pull the curtain to encircle the bed for privacy, though, as she told me, the two other beds were unoccupied, so for the time being I'd have the place to myself. She pointed out the bathroom across the hall, where there was a sink, a toilet, and a shower. The sight of each made me remember my mother cleaning the bathroom at the hospital after Olivia had left us to return to the campus—after Olivia had left, never to be invited into my life again, should I go ahead and keep the promise I'd made to my mother.

Sonny Cottler was with me at the infirmary and helped me move my belongings—textbooks and a few toilet items—so that, in keeping with the parting instructions from the doctor, I didn't have to carry or lift anything. Driving back from the hospital in the car, Sonny had said I could call on him for whatever I might need and invited me to the fraternity house for dinner that night. He was as kind and attentive as he could be, and I wondered if my mother had spoken to him about Olivia and if he was being so solicitous to prevent me from pining for her and breaking my deal with my mother or if he was secretly planning on calling her himself and taking her out again now that I had forsworn her. Even with him helping me, I couldn't get over my suspiciousness.

Everything I saw or heard caused my thoughts to turn to Olivia. I declined going to the fraternity house with Sonny and instead ate my first meal back on campus alone at the student cafeteria, hoping to find Olivia eating by herself at one of the smaller tables. To return to the infirmary, I took the long way around, passing the Owl, where I put my head inside to see if she might be eating by herself at the counter, even though I knew she disliked the place as much as I did. And all the while I went looking for an opportunity to run into her, and all the while I was discovering that everything, starting with the bathroom at the infirmary, reminded me of her, I was addressing her inside my head: "I miss you already. I'll always miss you. There'll never be anybody like you!" And intermittently, in response, came her melodic, lighthearted "I shot an arrow into the air / It fell to earth I knew not where." "Oh, Olivia," I thought, beginning to write her another letter, this too in my head, "you are so wonderful, so beautiful, so smart, so dignified, so lucid, so uniquely sexed-up. What if you did slit your wrist? It's healed, isn't it? And so are you! So you blew me—where's the crime? So you blew Sonny Cottler—where's . . ." But that thought, and the snapshot accompanying it, was not so easy to manage successfully and took more than one effort to erase. "I want to be with you. I want to be near you. You *are* a goddess—my mother was right. And who deserts a goddess because his mother tells him to? And my mother won't divorce my father no matter what I do. There is no way that she would send him to live with the cats in back of the store. Her announcing that she was divorcing him and had engaged an attorney was merely the ploy by which she tricked me. But then it couldn't be a ploy, since she'd already told me about divorcing him before she'd even known of you. Unless she'd already learned of you through Cottler's relatives in Newark. But my mother would never deceive me like that. Nor could I deceive her. I'm caught—I've made her a promise I can never break, whose keeping is going to break me!"

Or perhaps, I thought, I could fail to keep the promise without her finding out . . . But when I got to history class on Tuesday, any possibility of betraying my mother's trust disappeared, because Olivia wasn't there. She was absent from class on Thursday as well. Nor did I see her seated anywhere at chapel when I attended on Wednesday. I checked every seat in every row, and she wasn't there. And I had thought, We'll sit side by side through chapel, and everything that drives me crazy will suddenly be a source of amusement with Olivia enchantingly laughing beside me.

But she'd left school entirely. I had known it the moment I saw she was absent from history class, and had then confirmed it by calling her dormitory and asking to speak to her. Whoever picked up said, "She's gone home," politely, but in such a way as to make me think something had happened beyond Olivia's simply having "gone home"—something that none of them were supposed to talk about. When I did not call or contact her, she had tried again to kill herself—that had to be what had happened. After being called "Miss Hutton" a dozen times in twenty minutes by my mother, after waiting in vain for me to phone once I was back and settled into the infirmary, she had taken measures of just the kind my mother had warned me about. So I was lucky, was I not? Spared a suicidal girlfriend, was I not? Yes, and never before so devastated.

And what if she had not merely tried to kill herself—suppose she'd succeeded? What if she had slit both wrists this time, and bled to death in the dormitory—what if she had done it out at the cemetery where we had parked that night? Not only would the college do everything to keep it a secret, but so would her family. That way no one at Winesburg would ever know what happened, and no one but me would know why. Unless she'd left a note. Then everyone would blame her suicide on me—on my mother and on me.

I had to walk back to Jenkins and down to the basement, across from the post office, to find a pay phone with a folding door that I could tightly shut in order to make my call without anyone overhearing it. There was no note from her at the post office—that was what I'd checked first after Sonny had installed me in the infirmary. Before making my call, I checked again, and this time found there a college envelope containing a handwritten letter from Dean Caudwell:

Dear Marcus:

We're all glad to have you back on campus and to be assured by the doctor that you came through in top-notch shape. I hope now you'll reconsider your decision not to go out for baseball when spring comes. This coming year's team needs a rangy infielder, à la Marty Marion of the Cards, and you look to me as if you might well fill the bill. I suspect you're fast on your feet, and as you know, there are ways to get on base and help score runs that don't necessitate hitting the ball over the fence. A bunt dropped for a base hit can be one of the most beautiful things to behold in all of sports. I've already put in a word with Coach Portzline. He is eager to see you at tryouts when they're held on March 1. Welcome back rejuvenated to the Winesburg community. I like to think of this moment as your return to the fold. I hope you're thinking that way too. If I can be of any help to you, please do not hesitate to stop by the office.

> Yours sincerely,
> Hawes D. Caudwell,
> Dean of Men

I changed a five-dollar bill into quarters at the post office window, and then, after pulling shut the heavy glass door, I settled into the phone booth, where I arranged the quarters in stacks of four on the curved shelf beneath the phone in which a "G.L." had dared to carve his initials. Immediately I wondered how G.L. was disciplined when he was caught.

I was prepared for I didn't know what, and already as drenched in sweat as I had been in Caudwell's office. I dialed long-distance information and asked for Dr. Hutton in Hunting Valley. And there was such a one, a Dr. Tyler Hutton. I took down two numbers, for Dr. Hutton's office and for his residence. It was still daytime, and, having already convinced myself that Olivia was dead, I decided on calling the office, figuring that her father wouldn't be at work because of the death in the family, and that by speaking to a receptionist or a nurse I could get some idea of what had happened. I didn't want to speak to either of her parents for fear of hearing one or the other of them say, "So you're the one, you're the boy—you're the Marcus from her suicide note." After the long-distance operator reached the office number, and I had deposited a stream of quarters into the appropriate slot, I said, "Hello, I'm a friend of Olivia's," but didn't know what to say next. "This is Dr. Hutton's office," I was informed by the woman at the other end. "Yes, I want to find out about Olivia," I said. "This is the office," she said, and I hung up.

I walked directly down the Hill from the main quadrangle to the women's residence halls and up the stairs to Dowland Hall, where Olivia had lived and where I'd picked her up in Elwyn's LaSalle the night of the date that sealed her doom. I went inside, and at the desk blocking access to the first floor and the staircase was the student on duty. I showed her my ID and asked if she'd phone Olivia's floor to tell her that I was waiting downstairs. I'd already called Dowland on Thursday, when for the second time Olivia had failed to attend history class, and asked to speak to her. That's when I'd been told, "She's gone home." "When will she be back?" "She's gone home." So now I had asked for her again, this time in person, and again I was given the brushoff. "Has she gone for good?" I asked. The on-duty girl simply shrugged. "Is she all right, do you know?" She was a long time working up a response, only to decide in the end not to make one.

It was Friday, November 2. I was now five days out of the hospital and scheduled to resume climbing the three flights of stairs to my Neil Hall room on Monday, yet I felt weaker than I had when they got me up from bed to take my first few steps after the operation. Whom could I call to confirm that Olivia was dead without my also being accused of being the one who killed her? Would news of the death by her own hand of a Winesburg coed be in the papers? Shouldn't I go over to the library and comb through the Cleveland dailies to find out? The news surely wouldn't have been carried in the town paper, the *Winesburg Eagle*, or in the undergraduate paper, the *Owl's Eye*. You could commit suicide twenty times over on that campus and never make it into that insipid rag. What was I doing at a place like Winesburg? Why wasn't I back eating my lunch out of a paper bag down from the drunks in the city park with Spinelli and playing second for

Robert Treat and taking all those great courses from my New York teachers? If only my father, if only Flusser, if only Elwyn, if only Olivia—!

Next I rushed from Dowland back to Jenkins and hurried down the first-floor corridor to Dean Caudwell's office and asked his secretary if I could see him. She had me wait in a chair across from her desk in the outer office until the dean had finished meeting with another student. That student turned out to be Bert Flusser, whom I hadn't seen since I'd moved from the first of my rooms. What was he in with the dean for? Rather, why wasn't he with the dean every day? He must be in contention with him all the time. He must be in contention with *everybody* all the time. Provocation and rebellion and censure. How do you keep that drama going day in and day out? And who but a Flusser would want to be continually in the wrong, scolded and judged, contemptibly singular, disgusted by everyone and abominably unique? Where better than at Winesburg for a Bertram Flusser to luxuriate without abatement in an abundance of rebuke? Here in the world of the righteous, the anathema was in his element—more than could be said for me.

With no regard for the presence of the secretary,

Flusser said to me, "The puking—good work." Then he proceeded toward the door to the hallway, where he turned and hissed, "I'll be revenged on the whole pack of you." The secretary pretended to have heard nothing but merely rose to escort me to the dean's door, where she knocked and said, "Mr. Messner."

He came around from behind his desk to shake my hand. The stink I'd left behind me had long been eradicated by now. So how did Flusser know about it? Because everyone knew about it? Because the secretary to the dean of men had made it her business to tell them? This sanctimonious little piss-hole of a college—how I hated it.

"You look well, Marcus," the dean said. "You've lost a few pounds but otherwise you look fine."

"Dean Caudwell, I don't know who else to turn to about something that's very important to me. I never meant to throw up here, you know."

"You fell ill and you were sick and that's that. Now you're on the mend and soon will be yourself again. What can I do for you?"

"I'm here about a female student," I began. "She was in my history class. And now she's gone. When I told you I'd had one date, it had been with her.

Olivia Hutton. Now she's disappeared. Nobody will tell me where or why. I would like to know what happened to her. I'm afraid something terrible has happened to her. I'm afraid," I added, "that I may have had something to do with it."

You should never have said that, I told myself. They'll throw you out for contributing to a suicide. They could even turn you over to the police. They probably turned G.L. over to the police.

I still had in my pocket the dean's letter welcoming me back "rejuvenated" to the college. I'd only just picked it up. That's what had drawn me to his office—that's how foolishly I'd been taken in.

"What is it you did," he asked, "that makes you think this?"

"I took her out on a date."

"Did something happen on the date that you want to tell me about?"

"No, sir." He'd lured me in with no more than a kindly handwritten letter. *A bunt dropped for a base hit can be one of the most beautiful things to behold in all of sports. I've already put in a word about you with Coach Portzline. He's eager to see you at tryouts . . .* No, it was Caudwell who was eager to see me about Olivia. I had stepped directly into his trap.

"Dean," he said kindly. "I'm 'Dean' to you, please."

"The answer is no, Dean," I repeated. "Nothing happened that I want to tell you about."

"Are you sure?"

"Absolutely," and now I could imagine the suicide note and understood how I'd just been bamboozled into perjuring myself: "Marcus Messner and I had sexual contact and then he dropped me as though I were a slut. I'd prefer to be dead than live with that shame."

"Did you impregnate this young lady, Marcus?"

"Why—*no*."

"You're sure?"

"Absolutely sure."

"She wasn't pregnant as far as you know."

"No."

"You're telling the truth."

"Yes!"

"And you didn't force yourself on her. You didn't force yourself on Olivia Hutton."

"No, sir. Never."

"She visited you in your hospital room, did she not?"

"Yes, Dean."

"According to a member of the hospital staff, something occurred between the two of you at the hospital, something sordid occurred that was observed and duly recorded. Yet you say you didn't force yourself on her in your room."

"I'd just had my appendix out, Dean."

"That doesn't answer my question."

"I've never used force in my life, Dean Caudwell. On anyone. I've never had to," I added.

"You didn't have to. May I ask what that means?"

"No, no, sir, you can't. Dean Caudwell, this is very hard to talk about. I do think I have the right to believe that whatever may have happened in the privacy of my hospital room was strictly between Olivia and myself."

"Perhaps and perhaps not. I think everyone would agree that if it ever was strictly between the two of you, in the light of circumstances it isn't any longer. I think we would agree that's why you came to see me."

"Why?"

"Because Olivia is no longer here."

"Where is she?"

"Olivia had a nervous breakdown, Marcus. She had to be taken away by ambulance."

She who looked the way she looked was taken away in an ambulance? That girl so blessed with that brain and that beauty and that poise and that charm and that wit? This was almost worse than her being dead. The smartest girl around goes off in an ambulance because of a nervous breakdown while everybody else on this campus is taking stock of themselves in the light of biblical teachings and coming out feeling just fine!

"I don't really know what goes into a nervous breakdown," I admitted to Caudwell.

"You lose control over yourself. Everything is too much for you and you give way, you collapse in every conceivable way. You have no more control over your emotions than an infant, and you have to be hospitalized and cared for like an infant until you recover. If you ever do recover. The college took a chance with Olivia Hutton. We knew the mental history. We knew the history of electro-shock treatment and we knew the sad history of relapse after relapse. But her father is a Cleveland surgeon and a distinguished alumnus of Winesburg, and we took her in at Dr. Hutton's request. It didn't work out well either for Dr. Hutton or for the college, and it especially didn't work out for Olivia."

"But is she all right?" And when I asked the question I felt as though I were myself on the brink of collapsing. Please, I thought, please, Dean Caudwell, let us speak sensibly about Olivia and not about "relapse after relapse" and "electroshock"! Then I realized that was what he was doing.

"I told you," he said, "the girl had a breakdown. No, she is not all right. Olivia is pregnant. Despite her history, someone went ahead and impregnated her."

"Oh, no," I said. "And she's where?"

"At a hospital specializing in psychiatric care."

"But she can't possibly be pregnant too."

"She can and she is. A helpless young woman, a deeply unhappy person suffering from long-standing mental and emotional problems, unable adequately to protect herself against the pitfalls of a young woman's life, has been taken advantage of by someone. By someone with a lot of explaining to do."

"It's not me," I said.

"What was reported to us about your conduct as a patient at the hospital suggests otherwise, Marcus."

"I don't care what it 'suggests.' I will not be condemned on the basis of no evidence. Sir, I resent once again your portrayal of me. You falsify my motives and you falsify my deeds. I did not have sexual intercourse with Olivia." Flushing furiously I said, "I have never had sexual intercourse with anyone. Nobody in this world can be pregnant because of me. It's impossible!"

"Given all we now know," the dean said, "that's also hard to believe."

"Oh, fuck you it is!" Yes, belligerently, angrily, impulsively, and for the second time at Winesburg. But I *would* not be condemned on no evidence. I was sick of that from everyone.

He stood, not to rear back like Elwyn and take a shot at me but to let himself be seen in all his office's majesty. Nothing moved except for his eyes, which scanned my face as if in itself it were a moral scandal.

I left, and the wait to be expelled began. I couldn't believe Olivia was pregnant, just as I couldn't believe she'd sucked off Cottler or anyone else at Winesburg other than me. But whether or not it was true that she was pregnant—pregnant without telling me; pregnant, as it were, overnight; pregnant perhaps before she even got to Winesburg; pregnant, quite impossibly, like their Virgin Mary—I'd myself been drawn into the vapidity not merely of the Wines-burg College mores but of the rectitude tyranniz-ing my life, the constricting rectitude that, I was all too ready to conclude, was what had driven Olivia crazy. Don't look to the family for the cause, Ma— look to what the conventional world deems imper-missible! Look to me, so pathetically conventional upon his arrival here that he could not trust a girl because she blew him!

My room. My room, my home, my hermitage, my tiny Winesburg haven—when I reached it that Friday after a trek more laborious than I'd been ex-pecting up a mere three and a half flights of stairs, I found the bedsheets and blankets and pillows strewn in every direction and the mattress and the floor overspread with the contents of my dresser drawers, all of which were flung wide open. Under-shirts, undershorts, socks, and handkerchiefs were wadded up and scattered across the worn wooden floor along with shirts and trousers that had been pulled with their hangers from my tiny alcove of a closet and hurled everywhere. Then I saw—in the corner under the room's high little window—the garbage: apple cores, banana skins, Coke bottles, cracker boxes, candy wrappers, jelly jars, partially eaten sandwiches, and torn-off chunks of packaged bread smeared with what at first I took to be shit but was mercifully only peanut butter. A mouse appeared from amid the pile and scuttled under the bed and out of sight. Then a second mouse. Then a third.

Olivia. In a rage with my mother and me, Olivia had come to ransack and besmirch my room and then gone off to commit suicide. It horrified me to think that, crazed with rage as she was, she could have finished off this lunatic fiasco by slicing open her wrists right there on my bed.

There was a stink of rotting food, and another smell, equally strong, but one that I couldn't identify right off, so stunned was I by what I saw and surmised. Directly at my feet was a single sock turned inside out. I picked up the sock and held it to my nose. The sock, congealed into a crumpled mass, smelled not of feet but of dried sperm. Everything I then picked up and held to my nose smelled the same. Everything had been steeped in sperm. The hundred dollars' worth of clothing that

I'd bought at the College Shop had been spared only because they'd been on my back when I went off to the infirmary with appendicitis.

While I was away in the hospital somebody camping in my room had been masturbating day and night into almost every item I owned. And it wasn't, of course, Olivia. It was Flusser. It had to be Flusser. *I'll be revenged on the whole pack of you.* And this one-man bacchanalia was the revenge on me.

Suddenly I began to gag—as much from the shock as from the smells—and I stepped out the door to ask aloud of the empty corridor what harm I had done Bertram Flusser that he should perpetrate the grossest vandalism on my piddling possessions. In vain I tried to understand the enjoyment he had taken in defiling everything that was mine. Caudwell at one end and Flusser at the other; my mother at one end and my father at the other; playful, lovely Olivia at one end and broken-down Olivia at the other. And betwixt them all, I importunately defending myself with my fatuous fuck yous.

Sonny Cottler explained everything when he came for me in his car and I took him upstairs to show him the room. Standing in the doorway with me Sonny said, "He loves you, Marcus. These are tokens of his love." "The garbage too?" "The garbage especially," Sonny said. "The John Barrymore of Winesburg has been swept off his feet." "Is that true? Flusser's queer?" "Mad as a fucking hatter, queer as a three-dollar bill. You should have seen him in satin knee breeches in *School for Scandal*. Onstage, Flusser's hilarious—perfect mimic, brilliant farceur. Offstage, he's completely cracked. Offstage, Flusser's a gargoyle. There are such gargoyle people, Marcus, and you have now run into one." "But this isn't love—that's absurd." "Lots about love is absurd," Cottler told me. "He's proving to you how potent he is." "No," I said, "if it's anything, it's hatred. It's antagonism. Flusser's turned my room into a garbage dump because he hates my guts. And what did I do? I broke the goddamn record that he kept me up with all night long! Only that was weeks ago, that was back when I'd just got here. And I bought a new one—I went out the next day and replaced it! But for him to do a thing so huge and destructive and disgusting as this, that I should stick in his craw so much for so long— it makes no sense. You would think he was miles above caring about anybody like me—and instead, this clash, this quarrel, this loathing! What now? What next? How can I possibly live here anymore?" "You can't for now. We'll set you up tonight with a cot at the house. And I can loan you some clothes." "But look at this place, *smell* this place! He wants me to *wallow* in this shit! Christ, now I have to talk to the dean, don't I? I have to report this vendetta, don't I?" "To the dean? To Caudwell? I wouldn't advise it. Flusser won't go quietly, Marcus, if you're the one who fingers him. Talk to the dean and he'll tell Caudwell you're the man in his life. Talk to the dean and he'll tell Caudwell that you had a lover's spat. Flusser is our abominable bohemian. Yes, even Winesburg has one. Nobody can curb Bertram Flusser. If they throw Flusser out because of this, he'll take you down with him—that I guarantee. The *last* thing to do is to go to the dean. Look, first you're felled by an appendectomy, then all your worldly goods are bespattered by Flusser— of course you can't think straight." "Sonny, I cannot afford to get thrown out of school!" "But you haven't done anything," he said, closing the door to my stinking room. "Something was done to you."

But I and my animosity had done plenty, of

course, upon being charged by Caudwell with im-
pregnating Olivia.

I didn't like Cottler and didn't trust him, and the
moment I stepped into the car to take him up on
his offer of a cot and some clothes, I knew I was
making yet another mistake. He was glib, he was
cocky, he considered himself superior not just to
Caudwell but probably to me as well. A child of
the classiest Cleveland Jewish suburb, with long
dark lashes and a cleft in his chin, with two letters
in basketball and, despite his being a Jew, the president for the second straight year of the Interfraternity Council—the son of a father who wasn't a
butcher but the owner of his own insurance firm
and of a mother who wasn't a butcher either but the
heiress to a Cleveland department-store fortune—
Sonny Cottler was just too smooth for me, too self-
certain for me, quick and clever in his way but altogether the perfectly exemplary external young man.
The smartest thing for me to do was to get the hell
out of Winesburg and get myself back to New Jersey and, though it was already a third of the way
into the semester, try, before I got grabbed up by
the draft, to rematriculate at Robert Treat. Leave

the Flussers and the Cottlers and the Caudwells behind you, leave Olivia behind you, and head home
by train tomorrow, home where there is only a be-
fuddled butcher to deal with, and the rest is hardworking, coarse-grained, bribe-ridden, semi-xeno-
phobic Irish-Italian-German-Slavic-Jewish-Negro
Newark.

But because I was in a state, I went to the fraternity house instead, and there Sonny introduced me
to Marty Ziegler, one of the fraternity members, a
soft-spoken boy looking as though he hadn't yet required a shave, a junior from Dayton who idolized
Sonny, who would do anything Sonny asked, a born
follower to a born leader, who, up in the privacy of
Sonny's room, agreed on the spot, for only a buck
and a half a session, to be my proxy at chapel—to
sign my name on the attendance card, to hand it in
at the church door on the way out, and to speak to
no one about the arrangement, either while he was
doing it or after he'd completed the job. He had the
trusting smile of one possessed by the desire to be
found inoffensive by all, and seemed as eager to
please me as he was to please Sonny.

That Ziegler was a mistake, I was certain—the
final mistake. Not malevolent Flusser, the college

misanthrope, but kindly Ziegler—he was the destiny that now hung over me. I was amazed by what I was doing. No follower, either born or made, yet I too yielded to the born leader, after a day like this one, too exhausted and flabbergasted not to.

"Now," Sonny said, after my newly hired proxy had left the room, "now we've taken care of chapel. Simple, wasn't it?"

So said self-assured Sonny, though I knew without a doubt, even then, knew like the son of my fear-laden father, that this preternaturally handsome Jewish boy with a privileged paragon's princely bearing, used to inspiring respect and being obeyed and ingratiating himself with everyone and never quarreling with anyone and attracting the admiring attention of everyone, used to taking delight in being the biggest thing in his little interfraternity world, would turn out to be the angel of death.

It was already snowing heavily while Sonny and I were up in my room in Neil Hall, and by the time we'd reached the fraternity house, the wind had kicked up to forty miles an hour and, weeks before Thanksgiving, the blizzard of November '51 had

begun blanketing the northern counties of the
state, as well as neighboring Michigan and Indiana,
then western Pennsylvania and upstate New York,
and finally much of New England, before it blew
out to sea. By nine in the evening two feet of snow
had fallen, and it was still snowing, magically snowing, now without a wind howling through the
streets of Winesburg, without the town's old trees
swaying and creaking and their weakest limbs,
whipped by the wind and under the burden of
snow, crashing down into the yards and blocking
the roads and driveways—now without a murmur
from the wind or the trees, just the raggedy clots
swirling steadily downward as though with the intention of laying to rest everything discomposed in
the upper reaches of Ohio.

Just after nine we heard the roar. It carried all
the way from the campus, which lay about half a
mile up Buckeye Street from the Jewish fraternity
house where I'd eaten my dinner and been given a
cot and a dresser of my own—and some of Sonny's
freshly laundered clothes to put in it—and installed
as the great Sonny's roommate, for that night and
longer if I liked. The roar we heard was like the
roar of a crowd at a football game after a touch-

down's been scored, except that it was unabating. Like the roar of a crowd after a championship's been won. Like the roar that rises from a victorious nation at the conclusion of a hard-fought war.

It all began on the smallest scale and in the most innocently youthful way: with a snowball fight in the empty quadrangle in front of Jenkins among four freshman boys from small Ohio towns, boyish boys with rural backgrounds, who'd run out of their dormitory room to frolic in the first snowstorm of their first fall semester away at college. At the start, the underclassmen who rushed to join them emptied out of Jenkins only, but when residents in the two dorms perpendicular to Jenkins looked from their windows at what was happening in the quad, they began pouring from Neil, then from Waterford, and soon a high-spirited snowball fight was being waged by dozens of happy, hyperkinetic boys cavorting in dungarees and T-shirts, in sweatsuits, in pajamas, even some in only underwear. Within an hour, they were hurling at one another not just snowballs but beer cans whose contents they'd guzzled down while they fought. There were flecks of red blood in the clean snow from where some of them had been cut by the flying debris, which now included textbooks and wastebaskets and pencils and pencil sharpeners and uncapped ink bottles; the ink, cast wide and far, splotched the snow blue-black in the light of the electrified old gas lamps that gracefully lined the walkways. But their bleeding did nothing to dilute their ardor. The sight of their own blood in the white snow may even have been what provided the jolt to transform them from playful children recklessly delighting in the surprise of an unseasonable snowfall into a whooping army of mutineers urged on by a tiny cadre of seditious underclassmen to turn their rambunctious frivolity into stunning mischief and, with an outburst of everything untamed in them (despite regular attendance at chapel), to tumble and roll and skid down the Hill through the deep snow and commence a stupendous night out that nobody of their generation of Winesburgians would ever forget, one christened the next day by the *Winesburg Eagle*, in an emotionally charged editorial expressing the community's angry disgust, as "the Great White Panty Raid of Winesburg College."

They got inside the three girls' residence halls—Dowland, Koons, and Fleming—by bulling through the unplowed snow of the walkways and then on up the unshoveled stairs to the doorways and through the doors that were already shut tight for the night by breaking the glass to get to the locks or simply battering down the doors with fists, feet, and shoulders and tracking gobs of snow and churned-up slush inside the off-limits dormitories. Easily they overturned the on-duty desks that blocked access to the stairwells and then poured up onto the floors and into the bedrooms and sorority suites. While coeds ran in every direction in search of a place to hide, the invaders proceeded to fling open dresser drawer after dresser drawer, entering and sacking all the rooms to ferret out every pair of white panties they could find and to set them sailing out the windows and plummeting down onto the picturesquely whitened quadrangle below, where by now several hundred fraternity boys, who'd made their way out of the off-campus frat houses and through the deep drifts along Buckeye Street to the women's quad, had gathered to glory in this most un-Winesburgian wild spree.

"Panties! Panties! Panties!" The word, still as inflammatory for them as college students as it had been at the onset of puberty, constituted the whole of the cheer exultantly repeated from below, while up in the rooms of the female students the several scores of drunken boys, their garments, their hands, their crew-cut hair, their faces smeared blue-black with ink and crimson with blood and dripping with beer and melted snow, reenacted en masse what an inspired Flusser had done all on his own in my little room under the eaves at Neil. Not all of them, by no means anywhere close to all of them, just the most notable blockheads among them—three altogether, two freshmen and one sophomore, all of whom were among the first to be expelled the next day—masturbated into pairs of stolen panties, masturbated just about as quickly as you could snap your fingers, before each hurled the deflowered panties, wet and fragrant with ejaculate, down into the upraised hands of the jubilant gathering of red-cheeked, snow-capped upperclassmen breathing steam like dragons and egging them on from below.

Occasionally a single deep male voice, articulating in behalf of all those there unable to comply any longer with the prevailing system of moral discipline, baldly bellowed out the truth of it—"We want girls!"—but in the main it was a mob willing to settle for panties, panties that any number of them soon took to drawing down over their hair like caps or to pulling on up past their overshoes so as to sport the intimate apparel of the other gender atop their trousers as though they had dressed inside out. Among the myriad objects seen dropping from the open windows that night were brassieres, girdles, sanitary napkins, ointment tubes, lipsticks, slips and half slips, nighties, a few handbags, some U.S. currency, and a collection of prettily ornamented hats. Meanwhile, in the quadrangle yard, a large, breasted snowwoman had been built and bedecked in lingerie, a tampon planted jauntily in her lipsticked mouth like a white cigar, and finished off with a beautiful Easter bonnet arest atop a hairdo contrived from a handful of damp dollar bills.

Probably none of this would have happened had the cops been able to get to the campus before the innocuous snowballing out front of Jenkins had begun to veer out of control. But the Winesburg streets and the college paths wouldn't start to be cleared until the snowfall stopped, so neither the officers in the three squad cars belonging to the town nor the guards in the two campus security cars belonging to the college were able to make headway other than on foot. And by the time they reached the women's quad, the residences were a wreck and the mayhem was well beyond containment.

It took Dean Caudwell to stop some other, more grotesque outrage from occurring—Dean Caudwell standing six feet four inches tall on the front porch of Dowland Hall in his overcoat and muffler and calling through a bullhorn he grasped in his ungloved hand, "Winesburgians, Winesburgians, return to your rooms! Return immediately or risk expulsion!" It took that dire warning from the college's most revered and senior dean (and the fact that the draft was gobbling up eighteen-and-a-half-, nineteen-, and twenty-year-olds without college deferments) to begin to dispel the cheering mob of male students packed together into the women's quad and get them heading as quickly as they could back to wherever they'd come from. As for those inside the women's dorms still foraging through the dresser drawers, only when the town and the campus police entered and began hunting them down room by room did the last of the panties cease to drop from the windows—from windows all still wide open despite a nighttime temperature of twenty degrees—and only then did the invaders themselves begin to leap out the windows of the lower floors of Dowland, Koons, and Fleming into the cushion of deep snow accumulated below and, if they didn't break a limb in attempting their escape—as did two of them—to head for the Hill.

Later that night, Elwyn Ayers was killed. Being Elwyn, he'd had nothing to do with the panty raid, but after finishing his homework, he had (according to testimony provided by some half dozen of his fraternity brothers) spent the remainder of the evening back of the fraternity house, camped in his LaSalle, running the engine to keep it warm, and getting out only to sweep off the snow that rapidly settled on the roof, the hood, and the trunk and then to spade it away from the four wheels so he could attach a brand-new set of winter chains to the tires. For the sake of the automotive adventure, to see how well the powerful 1940 four-door Touring Sedan with the lengthened wheelbase and the larger carburetor and the 130 horsepower, the last of the prestigious cars named for the French explorer that GM would ever manufacture, could perform in the high-piled snow of the Winesburg streets, he decided to take it for a test spin. Downtown, where the railroad tracks had been kept clear by the stationmaster and his assistant throughout the storm, Elwyn attempted apparently to outrace the midnight freight train to the level crossing that separated Main Street from Lower Main, and the LaSalle, skidding out of control, spun twice around on the tracks and was struck head-on by the snowplow of the locomotive bound from points east to Akron. The car in which I had taken Olivia to dinner and then out to the cemetery—a historic vehicle, even a monument of sorts, in the history of fellatio's advent onto the Winesburg campus in the second half of the twentieth century—went careening off to the side and turned end-over-end down Lower Main until it exploded in flames, and Elwyn Ayers Jr. was killed, apparently on impact, and then quickly burned up in the wreckage of the car that he had cared for above all else in life and loved in lieu of men or women.

As it turned out, Elwyn was not the first, or even the second, but the third Winesburg senior who over the years since the introduction of the automobile into American life had failed to graduate because of having lost out in his attempt to outrace that midnight freight train. But he had taken the heavy snowfall for a challenge worthy of him and the LaSalle, and so, like me, my ex-roommate entered the realm of eternal recollection instead of the tugboat business, and here he will have forever to think about the fun of driving that great car. In my mind's eye I kept imagining the moment of impact, when Elwyn's pumpkin-shaped head crashed against the windshield and splattered very like a pumpkin into a hundred chunky pieces of flesh and bone and brain and blood. We had slept in the same room and studied together—and now he was dead at twenty-one. He had called Olivia a cunt—and now he was dead at twenty-one. My first thought on hearing of Elwyn's fatal accident was that I would never have moved had I known beforehand that he was going to die. Up until then, the only people I knew who had died were my two older cousins who'd been killed in the war. Elwyn was the first person who died that I hated. Must I now stop hating him to begin mourning him? Must I now start pretending that I was sorry to hear that he was dead, and horrified to hear how he had died? Must I put on a long face and go to the memorial service at his fraternity house and express condolences to his fraternity brothers, many of whom I knew as drunks who whistled through their fingers at me and called me something sounding suspiciously like "Jew" when they wanted service at the inn? Or should I try to reclaim residence in the room in Jenkins Hall before it wound up being assigned to somebody else?

"Elwyn!" I shout. "Elwyn, can you hear me? It's Messner! I'm dead too!"

Nothing in response. No, no roommates here. But then he wouldn't have replied anyway, the silent, violent, unsmiling prick. Elwyn Ayers, in death as in life, still opaque to me.

"Ma!" I shout next. "Ma—are you here? Dad, are you here? Ma? Dad? Olivia? Are any of you here? Did you die, Olivia? Answer me! You were the only gift Winesburg gave me. Who impregnated you, Olivia? Or did you finally end your life yourself, you charming, irresistible girl?"

But there is no one to speak to; there is only myself to address about my innocence, my explosions, my candor, and the extreme brevity of bliss in the first true year of my young manhood and the last year of my life. The urge to be heard, and nobody to hear me! I am dead. The unpronounceable sentence pronounced.

"Ma! Dad! Olivia! I am thinking of you!"

No response. To provoke no response no matter how painstaking the attempt to unravel and to be revealed. All minds gone except my own. No response. Profoundly sad.

The next morning, the *Winesburg Eagle*, in a "double" Saturday edition devoted entirely to all that the blizzard had unleashed at the college, reported that Elwyn Ayers Jr., class of '52, the sole fatality of the night, had in fact been the spark plug of the panty raid and had driven through the blinking red lights at the level crossing in an attempt to flee from discovery by the police—a completely cockeyed story and one retracted the following day, though not before it had been picked up and printed on page one of his hometown daily, the *Cincinnati Enquirer*.

Also that morning, promptly at seven A.M., the reckoning began on campus, with every underclassman who admitted to taking part in the panty raid furnished a snow shovel—the cost of which was tacked on to their semester's residence fees—and dragooned into snow-clearing squads whose task was to clear the campus roads and walkways of the thirty-four inches of snow that had been dumped by the blizzard and that in places had drifted to more than six feet. Each squad was overseen by upperclassmen on the university's athletic teams and the enterprise supervised by faculty members from the physical education department. At the same time, interrogations were conducted throughout the day in Caudwell's office. By nightfall eleven underclassmen, nine freshman and two sophomores, had been identified as ringleaders, and, having been denied the possibility of absolving themselves by doing penance on a snow removal crew (or of being punished with semester-long suspensions, as the families of the offenders were hoping would be the worst their young sons would be made to endure for what they tried to argue was no more than an undergraduate prank), they were permanently expelled from the college. Among them were the two who had broken limbs leaping from the women's residence halls and who had appeared before the dean in their fresh white casts, both, reportedly, with tears in their eyes and profuse apologies pouring from their lips. But they begged in vain for understanding, let alone for mercy. To Caudwell they were the two last rats fleeing the ship, and out they went for good. And anyone called before the dean who denied participating in the panty raid and who was subsequently discovered to be lying was summarily expelled as well, bringing the total expulsions to eighteen before the weekend was out. "You can't deceive me," Dean Caudwell told those called to his office, "and you won't deceive me." And he was right: nobody did. Not a one. Not even me in the end.

On Sunday evening, after supper, all Winesburg's male students were assembled in the lecture auditorium of the Williamson Lit. Building to be addressed by President Albin Lentz. It was from Sonny, as we tramped up to the Lit. Building that evening—all student cars having been banned from the still largely snow-covered town—that I learned about Lentz's political career and the speculation locally about his aspirations. He had been elected to two terms as a tough, strikebreaking governor of neighboring West Virginia before serving as an undersecretary in the War Department during World

War Two. After running unsuccessfully in that state for a U.S. Senate seat in '48, he'd been offered the presidency of Winesburg by business cronies on the college's board of trustees and arrived on the campus dedicated to making the pretty little college in north-central Ohio into what, in his inaugural address, he called "a breeding ground for the ethical propriety and the patriotism and the high principles of personal conduct that will be required of every young person in this country if we are to win the global battle for moral supremacy in which we are engaged with godless Soviet Communism." There were those who believed that Lentz had accepted the presidency of Winesburg, for which his qualifications were hardly those of an educator, as a steppingstone to the Ohio governorship in '52. If he succeeded, he would become only the second person in the country's history to have governed two states—both states heavily industrial—and thereby establish himself as a candidate for the Republican presidential nomination in '56 who could set out to break the Democrats' hold on their traditional working-class constituency. Among the students, of course, Lentz was known barely at all for his politics but instead for his distinctively rural twang—

he was the self-made son of a Logan County, West Virginia, miner—that penetrated his rotund oratory like a nail that then penetrated you. He was known for not mincing his words and for his ceaseless cigar smoking, a predilection that had earned him the campus epithet "the All-Powerful Stogie."

Standing not back of the lectern like a lecturing professor but solidly in front of it with his short legs set slightly apart, he began in an ominous interrogative mode. There was nothing bland about this man: he *had* to be listened to. He aspired not to cut a high-and-mighty figure like Dean Caudwell but to scare the wits out of the audience by his unbridled bluntness. His vanity was a very different sort of force from the dean's—there was no deficiency of intelligence in it. To be sure, he agreed with the dean that nothing was more serious in life than the rules, but his fundamental feelings of condemnation were delivered wholly undisguised (intermittent rhetorical embellishment notwithstanding). Never before had I witnessed such shock and solemnity—and fixed concentration—emanate from a congregation of the Winesburg student body. One could not imagine anyone present who even to himself dared to cry, "This is unseemly! This is not just!" The president could have come down into the auditorium and laid waste to the student assemblage with a club without inciting flight or stirring resistance. It was as though we already *had* been clubbed—and, for all the offenses committed, accepted the beating with gratification—before the assault had even begun.

Probably the lone student who had neglected to show up at a convocation of males billed as mandatory was that sinister free spirit, spite-filled Bert Flusser.

"Does any one of you here," President Lentz began, "happen to know what happened in Korea on the day all you he-men decided to bring disgrace and disrepute down upon the name of a distinguished institution of higher learning whose origins lie in the Baptist Church? On that day, U.N. and Communist negotiators in Korea reached tentative agreement for a truce line on the eastern front of that war-torn country. I take it you know what 'tentative' means. It means that fighting as barbaric as any we have known in Korea—as barbaric as any American forces have known in any war at any time in our history—that very same fighting can flare up any hour of the day or night and take thousands upon thousands more young American lives. Do any of you know what occurred in Korea a few weeks back, between Saturday, October 13, and Friday, October 19? I know that you know what happened here then. On Saturday the thirteenth our football team routed our traditional rival, Bowling Green, 41 to 14. The following Saturday, the twentieth, we upset my alma mater, the University of West Virginia, in a thriller that left us, the heavy underdogs, on top by a score of 21 to 20. What a game for Winesburg! But do you know what happened in Korea that same week? The U.S. First Cavalry Division, the Third Infantry Division, and my old outfit in the First War, the Twenty-fifth Infantry Division, along with our British allies and our Republic of Korea allies, made a small advance in the Old Baldy area. A small advance at a cost of four thousand casualties. Four thousand young men like yourselves, dead, maimed, and wounded, between the time we beat Bowling Green and the time we upset UWV. Do you have any idea how fortunate, how privileged, and how lucky you are to be here watching football games on Saturdays and not there being shot at on Saturdays, and on Mondays, Tuesdays, Wednesdays, Thursdays, Fridays, and Sundays as well? When measured against the sacrifices being made by young Americans of your age in this brutal war against the aggression of the North Korean and Chinese Communist forces —when measured against that, do you have any idea how juvenile and stupid and idiotic your behavior looks to the people of Winesburg and to the people of Ohio and to the people of the United States of America, who have been made aware by their newspapers and the television of the shameful happenings of Friday night? Tell me, did you think you were being heroic warriors by storming our women's dormitories and scaring the coeds there half to death? Did you think you were being heroic warriors by breaking into the privacy of their rooms and laying your hands on their personal belongings? Did you think you were being heroic warriors by taking and destroying possessions that were not your own? And those of you who cheered them on, who did not raise a finger to stop them, who exulted in their manly courage, what about *your* manly courage? How's it going to serve you when a thousand screaming Chinese soldiers come swarming down on you in your foxhole, should those negotiations in Korea break down? As they will, I can guarantee you, with bugles blaring and bearing their bayonets! What am I going to do with you boys? Where are the adults among you? Is there not a one of you who thought to *defend* the female residents of Dowland and Koons and Fleming? I would have expected a hundred of you, two hundred of you, three hundred of you, to put down this childish insurrection! Why did you not? Answer me! Where is your courage? Where is your honor? *Not a one of you displayed an ounce of honor! Not a one of you!* I'm going to tell you something now that I never thought I would have to say: I am ashamed today to be president of this college. I am ashamed and I am disgusted and I am enraged. I don't want there to be any doubt about my anger. And I am not going to stop being angry for a long time to come, I can assure you of that. I understand that forty-eight of our women students—which is close to ten percent of them—forty-eight have already left the campus in the company of their deeply shocked and shaken parents, and whether they will return I do not yet know. What I reckon from the calls I have been receiving from other

concerned families—and the phones in both my office and my home have not stopped ringing since
midnight on Friday—a good many more of our
women students are considering either leaving college for the year or permanently transferring out of
Winesburg. I can't say that I blame them. I can't say
that I would expect any daughter of mine to remain
loyal to an educational institution where she has
been exposed not merely to belittlement and humiliation and fear but to a genuine threat of physical harm by an army of hoodlums imagining, apparently, that they were emancipating themselves.
Because that's all you are, in my estimation, those
who participated and those who did nothing to stop
them—an ungrateful, irresponsible, infantile band
of vile and cowardly hoodlums. A mob of disobedi-
ent children. Kiddies in diapers unconstrained. Oh,
and one last thing. Do any of you happen to know
how many atom bombs the Soviets have set off
so far in the year 1951? The answer is two. That
makes a total of three atomic bombs altogether that
our Communist enemies in the USSR have now
successfully tested since they have discovered the
secret of producing an atomic explosion. We as a
nation are facing the distinct possibility of an un-

thinkable atomic war with the Soviet Union, all the while the he-men of Winesburg College are conducting their derring-do raids on the dresser drawers of the innocent young women who are their schoolmates. Beyond your dormitories, a world is on fire and you are kindled by underwear. Beyond your fraternities, history unfolds daily—warfare, bombings, wholesale slaughter, and you are oblivious of it all. Well, you won't be oblivious for long! You can be as stupid as you like, can even give every sign, as you did here on Friday night, of passionately *wanting* to be stupid, but history will catch you in the end. Because history is not the background—history is the stage! And you are *on* the stage! Oh, how sickening is your appalling ignorance of your own times! Most sickening of all is that it is just that ignorance that you are purportedly at Winesburg to expunge. What kind of a time do you think you belong to, anyway? Can you answer? Do you *know*? Do you have any idea that you belong to a time *at all*? I have spent a long professional career in the warfare of politics, a middle-of-the-road Republican fighting off the zealots of the left and the zealots of the right. But to me tonight those zealots are as nothing compared to you in your barbaric pursuit of thoughtless fun. 'Let's go crazy, let's have fun! How about cannibalism next!' Well, not here, gentlemen, not within these ivied walls will the delights of intentional wrongdoing go unheeded by those charged with the responsibility to this institution to maintain the ideals and values that you have travestied. This cannot be allowed to go on, and this *will* not be allowed to go on! Human conduct *can* be regulated, and it *will* be regulated! The insurrection is over. The rebellion is quelled. Beginning tonight, everything and everyone will be put back into its proper place and order restored to Winesburg. And decency restored. And dignity restored. And now you uninhibited he-men may rise and leave my sight. And if any of you decide you want to leave it for good, if any of you decide that the code of human conduct and rules of civilized restraint that this administration intends to strictly enforce to keep Winesburg Winesburg aren't suited to a he-man like yourself—that's fine with me! Leave! Go! The orders have been given! Pack up your rebellious insolence and clear out of Winesburg tonight!"

President Lentz had pronounced the words "thoughtless fun" as scornfully as if they were a synonym for "premeditated murder." And so conspicuous was his abhorrence of "rebellious insolence" that he might have been enunciating the name of a menace resolved to undermine not just Winesburg, Ohio, but the great republic itself.

Out from Under

Here memory ceases. Syrette after syrette of morphine squirted into his arm had plunged Private Messner into a protracted state of deepest unconsciousness, though without suppressing his mental processes. Since just after midnight, everything lay in limbo except his mind. Prior to the moment of cessation, to the moment when he was past recall and able to remember no more, the series of morphine doses had, in fact, infused the tank of his brain like so much mnemonic fuel while successfully dulling the pain of the bayonet wounds that had all but severed one leg from his torso and hacked his intestines and genitals to bits. The hilltop holes in which they'd been living for a week back of some barbed wire on a spiny ridge in central Korea had been overrun in the night by the

Chinese, and bodies in parts lay everywhere. When their BAR jammed he and Brunson, his partner, were finished—he'd not been encircled by so much blood since his days as a boy at the slaughterhouse, watching the ritual killing of animals in accordance with Jewish law. And the steel blade that sliced him up was as sharp and efficient as any knife they used in the shop to cut and prepare meat for their customers. Attempts by two corpsmen to stanch the bleeding and transfuse Private Messner were finally of no use, and brain, kidneys, lungs, heart—everything—shut down shortly after dawn on March 31, 1952. Now he was well and truly dead, out from under and far beyond morphine-induced recollection, the victim of his final conflict, the most ferocious and gruesome conflict of them all. They pulled his poncho over his face, salvaged the grenades in his web belt that he'd never had the chance to throw, and hurried back to Brunson, the next to expire.

In the struggle for the steep numbered hill on the spiny ridge in central Korea, both sides sustained casualties so massive as to render the battle a fanatical calamity, much like the war itself. The few whipped and wounded who hadn't been stabbed to death or blown apart eventually staggered off before first light, leaving Massacre Mountain—as that particular numbered hill came to be known in the histories of our midcentury war—covered with corpses and as void of human life as it had been for the many thousands of years before there arose a just cause for either side to destroy the other. In Private Messner's company alone, only twelve of two hundred survived, and not a one saved who wasn't crying and crazed, including the twenty-four-year-old captain in command, whose face had been crushed from the butt of a rifle swung like a baseball bat. The Communist attack had been launched by more than a thousand troops. The Chinese dead totaled between eight and nine hundred. They'd just kept coming and dying, advancing with bugles blaring "Arise, ye who refuse to be bondslaves!" and retreating through a landscape of bodies and blasted trees, machine-gunning their wounded and all they could locate of ours. The machine guns were Russian made.

In America the following afternoon, two soldiers came to the door of the Messner Newark flat to tell his parents that their only son had been killed in combat. Mr. Messner was never to recover from the news. In the midst of his sobbing he said to his wife, "I told him to watch out. He would never listen. You begged me not to double-lock the door in order to teach him a lesson. But you couldn't teach him a lesson. Double-locking the door taught him nothing. And now he's gone. Our boy is gone. I was right, Marcus, I saw it coming—and now you're gone forever! I cannot bear it. I will never survive it." And he didn't. When the store reopened after the period of mourning, he never joked lightheartedly with a customer again. Either he was silent while he worked, except for his coughing, or he said in a mumble to whomever he was serving, "Our son is dead." He stopped shaving regularly and no longer combed his hair, and soon, sheepishly, the customers started to drift away to find another kosher butcher in the neighborhood to frequent, and more of them took up shopping for their meat and their poultry at the supermarket. One day Mr. Messner was paying so little attention to what he was doing that his knife slipped on a bone and the tip of it entered his abdomen and there was a gush of blood and stitches were required. In all it took eighteen months for his horrendous loss to torture the wretched man to death; he died probably a decade before the emphysema would have grown acute enough to kill him on its own.

The mother was strong and lived on to be almost a hundred, though her life too was ruined. There was not a single day when she did not look at the high school graduation photograph of her handsome boy in its frame on the dining room sideboard and, aloud, ask in a sobbing voice of her late husband, "Why did you hound him out of the house? A moment's rage, and look what it did! What difference did it make what time he got home? At least he was home when he got here! And now where is he? Where are you, darling? Marcus, please, the door is unlocked—come home!" She went to the door then, the door with the notorious lock, and she opened it, opened it wide, and she stood there, knowing better, awaiting his return.

Yes, if only this and if only that, we'd all be together and alive forever and everything would work out fine. If only his father, if only Flusser, if only Elwyn, if only Caudwell, if only Olivia—! If only Cottler—if only he hadn't befriended the superior

Cottler! If only Cottler hadn't befriended him! If only he hadn't let Cottler hire Ziegler to proxy for him at chapel! If only Ziegler hadn't got caught! If only he had gone to chapel himself! If he'd gone there the forty times and signed his name the forty times, he'd be alive today and just retiring from practicing law. But he couldn't! Couldn't believe like a child in some stupid god! Couldn't listen to their ass-kissing hymns! Couldn't sit in their hallowed church! And the prayers, those shut-eyed prayers—putrefied primitive superstition! Our Folly, which art in Heaven! The disgrace of religion, the immaturity and ignorance and shame of it all! Lunatic piety about nothing! And when Caudwell told him he had to, when Caudwell called him back into his office and told him that they would keep him on at Winesburg only if he made a written apology to President Lentz for hiring Marty Ziegler to attend chapel in his stead and if thereafter he himself attended chapel not forty but, as a form of instruction as well as a means of penance, a total of eighty times, attended chapel virtually every single Wednesday for the remainder of his college career, what choice did Marcus have, what else could he do but, like the Messner that he was, like the student of

Bertrand Russell's that he was, bang down his fist on the dean's desk and tell him for a second time, "Fuck you"?

Yes, the good old defiant American "Fuck you," and that was it for the butcher's son, dead three months short of his twentieth birthday—Marcus Messner, 1932–1952, the only one of his classmates unfortunate enough to be killed in the Korean War, which ended with the signing of an armistice agreement on July 27, 1953, eleven full months before Marcus, had he been able to stomach chapel and keep his mouth shut, would have received his undergraduate degree from Winesburg College—more than likely as class valedictorian—and thus have postponed learning what his uneducated father had been trying so hard to teach him all along: of the terrible, the incomprehensible way one's most banal, incidental, even comical choices achieve the most disproportionate result.

Historical Note

In 1971 the social upheavals and transformations
and protests of the turbulent decade of the 1960s
reached even hidebound, apolitical Winesburg, and
on the twentieth anniversary of the November blizzard and the White Panty Raid an unforeseen uprising occurred during which the boys occupied the
office of the dean of men and the girls the office of
the dean of women, all of them demanding "student rights." The uprising succeeded in shutting
down the college for a full week, and afterward,
when classes resumed, none of the ringleaders of
either sex who had negotiated an end to the uprising by proposing liberalizing new alternatives to
the college officials were punished by expulsion or
suspension. Instead, overnight—and to the horror
of no authorities other than those by then retired

from administering Winesburg's affairs—the chapel requirement was abolished along with virtually all the strictures and parietal rules regulating student conduct that had been in force there for more than a hundred years and that were implemented so faithfully during the tradition-preserving tenure of President Lentz and Dean Caudwell.

ALSO BY PHILIP ROTH

THE FACTS

The Facts is an unconventional autobiography. Roth concentrates on five episodes from his life, including his passionate entanglement with the angriest person he ever met. The book concludes, in true Rothian fashion, with a sustained assault by the novelist against his proficiencies as an autobiographer.

Autobiography/Literature/978-0-679-74905-9

VINTAGE INTERNATIONAL
Available at your local bookstore, or visit
www.randomhouse.com